TIME ON THE HARBOUR

TIME ON THE HARBOUR

GRAHAM BOTTOMLEY

First published by Oceaniacom Press 2025
A division under Oceaniacom Pty Ltd.
www.oceaniacom.com

Time on the Harbour
Copyright © 2025 by GRAHAM BOTTOMLEY

ISBN (Print): 978-1-923113-14-5
ISBN (Ebook): 978-1-923113-15-2

Edited by Tim Humphries
Cover design by Clyde Cayetano

Acknowledgements

The front cover was designed by Clyde Cayetano from Concepts Agency capturing the mood and tone of *Time on the Harbour*.

Additionally, Chryssy Tintner and Susan B. Flanagan contributed to the *Time on the Harbour* screenplay, which this novella is based upon.

Thanks to Tim Humphries for his eagle-eyed edit.

Tribute

This story is a tribute to my beloved parents, Nell and Kevin Bottomley. The characters of Grandmother and Grandfather were inspired by my parents, who hold a special place in my heart. My father, a resident of 66 Forbes St Woolloomooloo, lived near Garden Island Naval Base from 1922 to 1934, and later worked on the nearby wharves. He courageously served in Papua, New Guinea during World War II, working as a gunner and wharf laborer.

My parents' selfless actions and dedication left a lasting impact on me. I will never forget the day my sister, Linda and I, were welcomed into their loving arms as mere infants. They chose to adopt us, and their unconditional love and care will forever remain etched in our memories. Dad's bravery and Mum's nurturing nature continue to inspire me every day. Their presence may no longer be physical, but their memory lives on in our hearts.

CONTENTS

CHAPTER 1

MAGIC

Bondi Public School playground was buzzing with kids running around and playing on 2 March 1999. The morning was warm, and the sun was shining bright, until a huge clap of thunder broke the tranquility. The kids stopped in their tracks and turned to see a blue pulsating swirl appearing from nowhere in the middle of the playground. They were all fascinated and curious, but also a little bit scared.

Suddenly, a man appeared from the swirl, as if by magic. The man was none other than Professor John Bentley, dandy in his late thirties, with an impressive Victorian-era moustache, top hat, and suit. He confidently strode across the playground, clutching a bespoke small suitcase that was exquisitely engraved with his name. He seemed to know exactly where he was headed, as he made his way towards a door marked "Cleaners."

All eyes were on him, including those of six-year-old boy, James Chang, who was standing nearby. James was fascinated by the man's outfit and decided to strike up a conversation.

"Hey mate," James said excitedly, "I like your outfit!"

Professor John Bentley stopped in his tracks, pondered for two beats, and then turned to face James. "Why, thank you!" he replied with a smile. "It's part of my magic act, dear boy."

James was even more intrigued now and asked, "You got a magic show today?"

The Professor nodded and replied, "Yes, it's a surprise, so." He moved closer to James and knelt, gesturing to him to keep quiet. "Can you keep a secret?" he asked with a mischievous glint in his eye.

"Yes, I'm the secretest," James replied, excited to be let in on a secret.

The Professor raised a single brow, as if weighing the boy's sincerity. Then, leaning even closer, he added with a touch of seriousness, "Promise? Don't say a thing to anyone. Cross your heart." His gaze locked on James's, steady and intent, as though this was a matter of utmost importance.

James nodded affirmatively and crossed his hand on his heart.

* * *

Twenty slightly bored sixth-grade students in a typical mid-90's classroom. Foppish teacher, Winslow Pedigrew, stands at a whiteboard littered with various Shakespeare quotes. Twelve-year-old, spick-and-span, Ben Upton, sits in the front row.

Winslow spruiks one of the Bard's best quips, "Hell is empty and all the devils are here." He raises his eyebrows and theatrically gestures to the class.

Ben retorts, "I prefer Kylie Minogue's, 'Better the Devil You Know.'"

Winslow quickly responds, "That quip is actually a shortened version of a 13th Century Irish proverb."

Ben snaps back, "Well, I like Kylie's short shorts."

The class holds back laughter. Professor Winslow glares at Ben who has a mischievous glint in his eye, the class still holding back their laughter, Ben's mind was already racing with ideas for his next comeback.

"Okay, Mr. Upton. You can see the Principal for that insolence," Winslow said with a playful smile.

A forlorn Ben rose with his backpack and marched towards the door, but he couldn't help but smile to himself knowing he had impressed Professor Winslow and his class with his quick wit.

* * *

As Professor John Bentley, now donned in janitor's attire in the Cleaners Room, checks the time on his antique pocket watch, he takes a deep breath and prepares for the task ahead. With a determined look in his eyes, he counts down silently, "Three...two...one..." and pushes open the door, cart in tow.

Making his way down the long corridor, Professor John Bentley catches sight of Ben, sauntering along with his backpack slung over his shoulder. With precision, the Professor aims his cart at the backpack and knocks it from Ben's grip, causing the books to scatter across the floor.

"Oops, my apologies, dear boy," Professor John Bentley says with a hint of mischief in his voice.

As Ben scrambles to pick up his books, the Professor slyly slips a book from his cart into the backpack. "It's alright, mister. My day was already terrible anyway," Ben mutters, trying to gather his things.

"Please forgive my clumsiness, dear chap," Professor John Bentley says with a hint of guilt in his tone.

With a nod, Ben collects his belongings and continues down the corridor, unaware of the secret exchange that just took place.

Professor John Bentley steps out of the Cleaners door, adorned in his 19th Century finery and clutching his suitcase. As he strides across the playground, he is met by James who has just emerged from the boy's bathroom. The boy's eyes are wide with excitement as he asks if he missed the magic show. With a twinkle in his eye, Professor John Bentley confirms that he did indeed miss it. James is visibly upset, but the Professor leans down to pat him on the head and offers to do the finale for him. James nods eagerly, his disappointment quickly fading.

The Professor surveys the playground, ensuring that no one is watching. He then pulls out a small retro futuristic machine from his bag and presses a button before heading towards the school gate.

"Blast me from Bondi!" the Professor exclaims as he disappears into a blue pulsating swirl that has appeared in the playground.

James watches in awe as the Professor calmly walks into the swirl and vanishes. He can't believe what he has just witnessed and runs to the spot where the Professor disappeared, shouting, "Blast me from Bondi!" in hopes of experiencing the same magic. However, nothing happens. James looks up at the sky and jumps twice, but still nothing.

Disappointed, he lets out a sigh and walks back to the bathrooms, wondering if he will ever be able to witness such amazing magic again. Little does he know; this is just the beginning of adventures thanks to the mysterious Professor John Bentley.

***

Ben's eyes widen as he becomes completely immersed in the pages of *The Time Machine* book in the sanctity of his modest Bondi bedroom. He is transported to another world, filled with futuristic technology and thrilling adventures. The words seem to jump off the page, bringing the story to life in his mind. He can't believe that such a small book could hold so much magic within its pages. As he turns the pages, Ben can't help but feel a sense of wonder and excitement. He imagines himself as the main character, traveling through time and experiencing unimaginable things.

Suddenly, he hears a loud noise and jumps up from the couch, thinking it was a sound from the book. But as he looks around, he realizes it was just a car passing by outside.

Disappointed, Ben lets out a sigh and closes the book. He can't believe that he was so engrossed in the story, only to be brought back to reality so abruptly. He walks back to the bathroom, his mind still buzzing with the incredible world he had just experienced. Little does he know; this is just the beginning.

***

17 MAY 2007

The sound of crashing waves fills the air as the sun sets over iconic Sydney Harbour. The water glistens with a golden hue, creating a serene and picturesque setting. Suddenly, the peacefulness is shattered as a jet ski roars into view. The rider, Professor Bentley, cuts through the water with expert precision. He is in his late thirties, with a ruggedly handsome face and a determined gaze. His wet-suit clings to his muscular frame, highlighting his athleticism.

In one swift movement, he stops the jet ski about 100 metres offshore. He reaches into a backpack and pulls out his phone. The screen reads: *"SYDNEY MORNING HERALD HEADLINE - WILD STORMS TO HIT SYDNEY."* A look of concern crosses his face as he glances towards the darkening sky. But his attention is soon drawn to something else in the backpack—a small, retro-futuristic machine. With careful precision, he reveals the glass encased device, adorned with chrome dials and diodes. A small plaque reads: *"Temporal Change Device."* Without hesitation, he sets the analogue dial to 7:05 PM, 30 May 1942. With a determined look, Professor Bentley stands and drops the device into the water, next to a tide marker pole. It floats for a few seconds before sinking beneath the surface. As he watches it disappear, a mix of emotions crosses his face—determination, hope, and perhaps a hint of fear.

Bentley revs the jet ski and speeds towards the shore, leaving behind a trail of foamy waves. His mind is undoubtedly filled with thoughts of the past, the future, and the consequences of his actions. This is not a simple man on a simple mission. He is a man of mystery, complexity, and perhaps even a little danger. And as he disappears into the horizon, the sky darkens and the wind picks up, foreboding the wild storms that are about to hit Sydney.

As the storm clouds roll in over the Harbour, all hell breaks loose in the sky. Lightning and thunder strike with epic proportions, causing chaos and destruction in their wake.

The beach is no exception, as repeated bolts of lightning strike the trees, bushes, and sand. The sound of the storm is deafening, and the force of nature is truly a sight to behold. As the bolt of lightning hits the tide marker, setting it ablaze, something incredible happens underwater. Tracing the bolt's path down the pole, it sparks onto the *Temporal Change Device* wedged into a crevice near the pole. The machine lights up, its dials and parts revolving as a blue glow surge from it into the water. And above the surface, the glow can be seen spreading below for several metres, as the storm sound fades into the background.

CHAPTER 2

EXPOSED

BONDI BEACH - THE NEXT DAY

The morning sun casts a golden hue over the crystal blue ocean. The sound of crashing waves echoes through the air. A group of ten surfers jockey for position in the glassy swell, their boards gliding effortlessly through the water.

Downstream, nineteen-year-old lone surfer Mark Bentley, paddles frantically, his muscles straining against the powerful current. Disheveled and Adonis-like, he radiates determination and confidence. With a sudden burst of energy, he jumps upright and catches the perfect wave.

Mark's smirk turns into a wide grin as he savors his ride in the two-meter swell. He moves with the grace and precision of a seasoned surf pro, effortlessly riding the wave with expert skill. But just as he starts to relax into the rhythm of the ocean,

Mark suddenly loses balance and footing. His arms flail as he takes an awkward dive, disappearing beneath the crashing water. Panic sets in as he tumbles around, disoriented and struggling to find his way back to the surface. For a moment, all is chaos and turmoil under the water. But then, with a burst of strength and determination, Mark breaks through the surface, gasping for air. His hair is plastered to his face, and his chest heaves with exertion. But despite his struggle, his eyes are alight with a fierce determination to conquer the waves.

Mark's body plunged into the sand, his face contorting in panic. The sound of thrashing water and frantic gasps for air filled the beach as he searched desperately for his missing board shorts. Bubbles escaped his mouth, and his arms flailed wildly in a feverish attempt to locate the elusive garment. Underwater, Mark's voice was a garbled mess of incoherent shouts. He bounced up and down like a jack-in-the-box, his movements becoming more frenzied with each passing second. Finally, Mark broke through the surface, gasping for breath like a drowning man. His eyes scanned the shoreline in a desperate attempt to find his beloved boardies.

"Shit!" he cursed; his frustration evident in his voice. "My boardies! Where are they?" He treaded water, his body twisting and turning as he frantically searched the water's surface. His gaze darted back and forth, his mind racing with thoughts of how he could have lost his prized possession. But as he looked back at the beach, his expression changed from one of panic to one of intense determination. Mark's character was complex, and his emotions ran deep. He was not one to give up easily, he dove back into the water, determined to find his missing shorts no matter what it took.

The blistering sun beat down on the sandy beach, casting a bright glare over the shore. Mark's board shorts, a vibrant shade of blue, were gently washed up to shore by the lapping waves. Rachel and Kate, two alluring and athletic seventeen-year-old girls, jogged along the shoreline, their toned bodies glistening with sweat. As they approached the board shorts, Rachel's eyes lit up with mischievous delight.

She picked them up and held them up to Mark, who stood waist-deep in the water, his face flushed with embarrassment.

Rachel yells, "Hey there, grommie. Are these yours?"

"Yeah, can you just throw them over," replies Mark.

Rachel took a few steps back, her friends joining in with her laughter. She shook her head playfully. "Sorry, I can't do that. You're going to have to come get them."

Mark's frustration was clear as he stood up in the water, his naked body on display. Kate couldn't help but admire his chiseled physique, but Rachel pretended not to be impressed.

Kate leaned into whisper to Rachel, "Oh my god, he's so hot." Rachel brushed her off, her eyes scanning Mark up and down.

A shaken Mark says, "How would you feel, buck naked? They came off when I wiped out."

Rachel boasts, "Well, my brother is about the same size as you—in build, I mean. He could use a new pair of boardies."

With a playful smirk, Rachel turned and started to jog away, her friend Kate following close behind.

Mark was left standing in the water, feeling both embarrassed and intrigued by the captivating girls who had just crossed his path.

The tranquil waves of the ocean gently kiss the shore as a group of Japanese tourists arrive at the promenade. Excited chatter and the sound of camera shutters fill the air. Amidst the commotion, a rebellious Japanese teenage girl, fifteen years old, spots Mark through her camera lens. She exclaims, "Look, that attractive man is completely nude!".

Curious, a teenage boy from the group turns to look, and yells, "Where? I don't see anything."

The girl points, "Right there, blind boy. He's completely exposed!"

The Japanese women on the bus quickly turn their cameras towards Mark. Even an elderly Japanese lady, with a mischievous twinkle in her eye, aims her camera at him, and seductively sighs, "Oh my, what a beautiful bum! Come on, turn around, turn around. Yes, he's turning!"

A smile spreads across her face as the other women giggle and join in on the fun.

Mark slowly turns and strides towards Rachel, the water reaching up to his knees. His hands are strategically placed in front of his groin, trying to maintain some modesty.

Rachel stands still, about five meters away from him, holding his board shorts teasingly in front of her. She playfully asks for his name.

Mark responds with a hint of embarrassment, "Mark."

Rachel smirks and taunts, "Well, Mark, it looks like you'll have to come and get your boardies."

Mark pleads, "You wouldn't be so cruel."

Rachel's eyes twinkle mischievously as she asks, "Little ol' me? Or should I say, little ol' you?"

Mark reluctantly starts to move closer to the girls, still trying to cover himself. He can feel the heat rising in his cheeks from the awkward situation. Rachel can't contain her laughter as she tosses the board shorts to Mark. He jumps up, reaching out to catch them, his face full of relief and gratitude.

On the promenade, an aging Japanese woman gazes intently through her camera's lens, watching as Mark takes a leap and the girls erupt into a chorus of joyful screams.

The elderly lady whispers, "Shake it, honey! Shake it like a polaroid!" The staccato snap of multiple cameras and the tinkling laughter of youth fills the air.

As Mark snatches the board shorts mid-air, he hastily covers his groin. Rachel and Kate observe with rapt attention, their arms crossed. A mischievous smile plays on their faces, reveling in their voyeuristic tendencies.

Rachel wryly says, "The water must be frigid today."

As Mark stumble, he slips on his board shorts. He quickly regains his balance, pretending nothing happened.

Rachel yells, "We should get going now. Nice to meet you, Mark. Hopefully, we'll catch more of you."

Mark mutters under his breath, "Is there anything left to reveal?"

With a nonchalant saunter, Rachel walks away without a second glance.

The mature Japanese woman sets down her camera and turns towards the rebellious Japanese girl. The older lady exclaims, "This beats koalas pissing from trees!"

Gemma Bentley, Mark's sister, skates past the elderly woman. Gemma, at the age of seventeen, is drop dead gorgeous. The old woman gazes at Gemma as she skates by.

Every man on the boardwalk and beach also takes notice of her, moving along to the beat of her iPod. Gemma wears form-fitting shorts, a sheer white top, and radiates a captivating, flawless smile. Everyone she passes is captivated by her presence.

As Gemma is approached by Jason, a suave twenty-eight-year-old, and his two burly henchmen, she is flagged down. Jason, wearing a sly grin, would have no qualms about selling out his own grandmother. Gemma halts and removes her headphones upon Jason's request.

"May I help you?" Gemma inquires.

"As a matter of fact, you can, honey. I'm Jason. And what may I call you?" Jason responds with confidence as he reaches out to shake her hand.

Gemma cautiously extends her hand in return. "Gemma," she says.

"Hello, Gemma. I happen to own a brand-new nightclub in Bondi Junction. And I would like to invite you to our grand opening!" Jason smoothly retrieves a business card and an invitation from his pocket, then hands them to Gemma.

"Let me guess. It's a hip-hop club, right?" Gemma knowingly remarks.

"Yes! It's what everybody wants. And what do *you* want?" Jason slides closer to Gemma. She instinctively takes a step back and furrows her brow.

The shore is bustling with activity. Now nineteen-year-old Ben Shipton, who has a round physique, tosses a Roosters Rugby League football to his friend, eighteen-year-old Dan..

They are joined by two other mates, and together they form a circle on the sandy shore. Surfboards, towels, and other beach essentials surround them.

"That's Gemma," Ben remarks, gesturing to her as she walks on the promenade. "Who's the other guy?" Distracted by Gemma and another person, Ben turns his attention away from the group.

On the promenade, confident Jason stands before a nervous Gemma. Behind him, his thuggish friends loom menacingly. Back on the shore, Ben notices Gemma's reaction to Jason and feels apprehensive.

Dan and their friends wait nearby. "Hey mate, it looks like she's in trouble," Dan says, nodding towards Gemma. "You should go check it out and make sure she's okay."

Ben hesitates and looks uncertainly at Dan. "Should I?" he asks.

"Of course, do it man," Dan insists. "She's Mark's sister, and he's your mate."

Reluctantly, Ben agrees and begins to make his way towards Gemma.

Ben cautiously approaches Gemma, but quickly glances at his companions. Jason looms over Gemma, his cronies lurking in the background. Behind them, Ben clears his throat to get their attention, but his efforts go unheard.

"Excuse me!" he calls out, raising his voice.

Gemma whips around, surprised to see Ben.

"Ben?" she gasps.

He nods, his voice trembling. "It's me. Ben."

Jason steps forward, eyeing Ben suspiciously. "Do you have something to say, mate?" he asks, his cronies moving in closer with questioning expressions. Undeterred, Jason confidently steps up to Ben.

Clearing his throat once more, Ben speaks up. "Just wanted to make sure you were alright," he says.

"What's that?" Jason taunts. "We can't hear you."

"Don't worry, Ben," Gemma interjects. "I'm fine."

The cronies puff out their chests, intimidating Ben. Gemma lunges forward, but Jason holds her back. One of the thugs' shoves Ben, causing him to stumble and fall onto the sand.

"What's wrong with you?" Gemma demands. "Why did you do that?"

Jason smirks. "As I said, Gemma, I want to invite you to my nightclub."

On the sand now, Ben reaches for his phone and dials quickly. "Mark, it's Ben," he says through gritted teeth. He winces as he rubs his sore backside.

Mark's phone rings, interrupting his peaceful morning at the beach. Standing by his board, he answers casually, "Hey Ben, what's doin?"

Ben's voice crackles through the phone. "Listen Mark, your sister's in trouble."

Mark's expression shifts, his relaxed stance turning into a frown. He glances around the beach, taking in the sun and the sound of the waves crashing against the shore. "What's happened?" he asks, trying to stay calm.

Ben's voice becomes urgent, "These guys are talking to her. Hassling her. They're super creepy."

Mark's eyes narrow, his grip on his phone tightening. He scans the promenade, trying to spot his sister among the crowd. "Did they hurt her?" he asks, his voice tinged with concern.

"No..." Ben's voice trails off.

Mark sighs, his relaxed stance returning. "Ben, she's fronted by dudes all the time. Gemma can look after herself," he says with certainty, convinced that his sister can handle whatever situation she's in.

But Ben is not convinced. He stands up and waves his arms, trying to get Mark's attention. "You're not even going to help her?" he yells through the phone.

Mark's expression turns to confusion. "Look, if she's not in danger, then why should I?" he retorts.

Ben scolds him, "Man, you don't care about your own sister! In fact, you don't seem to care about your girlfriends either. You treat them like dirt, dude!"

Mark is taken aback, his phone still pressed against his ear. He tries to calm Ben down, "Okay, okay man, calm down. So, what's happening now?" he asks, standing over his board with his towel and clothes in hand.

Ben's eyes widened as he watched Gemma's body language. She was giggling and playfully touching Jason and his two muscle-bound companions. She grabbed Jason's bicep and squeezed it tightly, her laughter ringing out like a siren. Ben's jaw clenched as he tried to make sense of the situation. Why was Gemma acting like this? Who were these guys and why was she flirting with them?

As he stood on the shore of Bondi Beach, Mark's voice broke through his thoughts.

"So, everything's okay, yeah?" Mark asked knowingly, already aware of the situation.

Ben's thoughts raced and he felt a pang of guilt. "Yeah, I panicked when those guys surrounded her. Sorry for what I said before," he replied regretfully.

Mark let out a laugh. "Don't worry about it, mate. Are you still up for snorkeling tomorrow?"

Ben's mind shifted to a more positive thought. "Yeah, for sure," he replied with a smile.

"Great, see you then," Mark said as he put his phone away, leaving Ben to face the situation at hand.

Taking a deep breath, Ben headed towards Gemma, who was still flirting with Jason. As he approached, she turned to him with a smile. "You okay, Benny?" she asked, her voice filled with concern.

Ben's heart softened at her words. "Yeah, I must have misread the situation," he admitted.

Gemma's smile widened. "Aw, that's sweet. You were worried about me!"

Jason, who had been watching the exchange, spoke up. "Sorry about my friends, mate. They're just very overprotective."

Ben shook his head, trying to brush off the awkwardness. "Just a misunderstanding. No worries."

Gemma leaned in and gave him a quick hug. "See ya, Benny," she said before turning back to Jason.

CHAPTER 3

PIVOTAL

Ben enters the Bentley house, greeted by the sight of a worn, silver-haired man. This is Kevin "Butch" Bentley, eighty-four years old and the grandfather of Mark and Gemma. He opens the door with a smile, inviting Ben inside.

"Come in, son," he says warmly. "Mark and Gem are waiting for you."

Ben steps into the hallway, taking in the old photographs and decorations that line the walls. His eyes fall upon a particular photo, a snapshot of a young Butch at nineteen, posing proudly with fellow soldiers in their WWII uniforms.

Ben's curiosity is piqued, and he turns to Butch. "Where was this taken, Mr. Bentley?" he asks.

Butch's face softens as he remembers the past, "*H.M.A.S. Kuttabul,*" he replies. "Before it was torpedoed by the Japs in '42." He was known as "Butch" back then.

A sudden concern washes over Ben's face, "Were you on board?" he asks.

Butch shakes his head, "No, thank Christ. I was one of the lucky ones."

Ben can't help but ask, "What happened?"

Butch runs a hand through his silver-grey hair, his eyes clouding with memories, "I was walking home." And with that, he begins his story. The details are vivid and raw, the emotions intense as Butch relives the events of that fateful day. The smell of the sea air, the fear and adrenaline coursing through his veins. Ben is captivated, transported to a time he can only imagine.

"It was a humid day in Woolloomooloo, 1942. I was a young man of nineteen and strolled down the street in my WWII uniform. I turned into an alley, the sound of my footsteps echoing off the walls. Suddenly, two rough looking muggers appeared from the shadows, their faces twisted into menacing sneers. Without warning, I was struck with a large two by four, sending me crashing to the ground.

"The muggers wasted no time in unleashing a brutal assault, their fists and feet raining down on my body. The pain was excruciating, but I couldn't even cry out as the blows landed. As I lay on the ground, my vision blurred and head spinning, I could hear the muggers rifling through my pockets. I knew they were taking my wallet, the one thing of value I had had on me. I was helpless, unable to stop them from robbing me. With my wallet now in their possession, the muggers sprinted away down the alley, leaving me battered and bruised. I moaned in pain, feeling like a sack of potatoes that had been mercilessly beaten.

"The world around me faded as I slipped into unconsciousness. In that moment, my thoughts were not on the physical pain or the loss of the wallet. Instead, I was overwhelmed by a sense of betrayal and injustice. These were not just muggers; they were heartless bastards. And as I drifted into darkness, I vowed to never let anyone do that again."

As Ben listened to Kevin's story, he could feel the intensity in Kevin's voice. The events leading up to the assault were already horrifying, but what came next was even more shocking, "I was left unconscious and alone in a pool of my own blood for twenty agonizing minutes. It was clear that these were not just ordinary muggers, but heartless individuals who had taken advantage of me.

"As I lay there, my thoughts were consumed with a sense of betrayal and injustice. This was a moment that would shape my life forever."

Ben imagined Kevin in the Woolloomooloo alley, laying motionless in a pool of blood.

Kevin continued, "A young couple, Jess and Tim, walked by, their carefree laughter quickly turned into disbelief. They were shocked to see the state I was in and at once rushed to my aid. Tim, being a soldier, knew the severity of the situation and quickly took charge. As Jess ran off to get help, Tim knelt beside me, trying to assess the situation. My condition was dire, and it was clear that I needed urgent medical attention.

"Tim's thoughts raced as he held my head, hoping that help would arrive soon. As Jess made her way to Garden Island for help, her mind was consumed with the image of me lying in that alley. She couldn't believe the cruelty of the world and the heartlessness of those who had attacked me. The shock of the incident had shaken her to her core, and she couldn't wait to get help for me. Little id she know this encounter would change my life."

Ben watched in awe as Kevin recounted his harrowing experience. "Are you alright?" Ben asked, concern etched on his face.

"Yeah, I recovered in a few weeks," Kevin replied, trying to sound nonchalant.

But, Ben could sense there was more to the story. "What happened?" Ben prodded; his curiosity piqued.

"Well, that night I was supposed to be on the *Kuttabul*, but I ended up in the hospital instead," Kevin began. "And thank God for that, because the Japs torpedoed the boat, and twenty-one men lost their lives."

Ben's eyes widened in shock, "So, the beating actually saved your life?"

Kevin nodded with a wry grin. "I owe those two thugs my life. If it wasn't for them, I'd be six feet under."

"That's insane!" Ben exclaimed, hardly able to believe it.

"Insane is an understatement, kid," Kevin replied with a hint of bitterness. "That beating was the only thing that saved me from a watery grave."

As Kevin spoke, Ben could feel the weight of the setting pressing down on him. The dimly lit room, the musty smell of old books, and the sounds of the nearby Bondi waves outside all added to the intensity of the story. But it was Kevin's words and the emotion behind them that truly brought the scene to life. Ben could almost feel the fear and desperation Kevin must have felt on that fateful night. And as he looked at the scarred man sitting in front of him, he couldn't help but admire his strength and resilience.

* * *

THE NEXT DAY

The door swung open, and Ben sauntered in, an iced coffee in hand. Gemma and Mark, dressed in vibrant beach gear, looked up from their conversation. Without a word, Ben and Mark bump chests, their firm grip reflecting a sense of camaraderie.

"Hey," Ben said casually, taking a sip of his iced coffee. "Your Pop told me about that time he got into a fight that saved his life."

Mark shrugged; his expression uninterested. "Yeah, we've heard it a thousand times. Couldn't care less."

Ben furrowed his brow, intrigued. "What's your deal with your Gramps?"

Mark's gaze drifted down the hallway, his eyes vacant. "We don't have anything in common. And besides..." His voice trailed off, lost in thought.

The warm sun streamed in through the open windows, filling the room with a bright glow. The faint sound of seagulls could be heard in the distance, creating a peaceful atmosphere. The scent of sunscreen and salty ocean air wafted through the air, evoking a sense of carefree summer days.

"Seriously ,though," Ben pressed on, breaking the tranquil scene. "What's the story with you two?"

Mark let out a heavy sigh, his shoulders slumping. "It's complicated," he finally said, his voice tinged with emotion.

* * *

NINE YEARS EARLIER, 1998

The scene was chaotic, with emergency workers rushing around a tent set up next to the wreckage of two SUVs. Smoke billowed out of the mangled Hyundai; its engine destroyed in the violent crash.

On the curb, a larger SUV sat, its front-end smashed in. Emergency service vehicles filled the lane, while a barricade forced traffic to squeeze into one lane, herded by a stern cop.

During the chaos, a young boy, Mark, and his sister, Gemma, arrived in a Corolla driven by a middle-aged woman. Mark's eyes immediately locked onto the smoking Hyundai and he made a break for it. But a young male constable held him back, while Gemma sat trembling in the backseat, her hand over her mouth in horror.

She looked around, trying to make sense of what was happening. "Mummy? Daddy?" Gemma's trembling voice broke through the chaos.

Meanwhile, Mark listened intently as his grandfather, Kevin, spoke to a female cop, Sergeant Bryant. The tension was profound as they discussed what had happened.

"So, you were speaking to your son on the phone and heard screeching brakes, then crunching metal before the phone went dead?" Sergeant Bryant asked, looking at her clipboard.

Kevin reluctantly nodded.

"We found a mobile near the accident scene. The last incoming call was from: 0414 637 972. Is that your number?" Sergeant Bryant's words hung in the air, causing Kevin to shift uncomfortably.

"Yes, Officer. It looks like I phoned him just before he crashed." Kevin's voice was heavy with guilt.

Suddenly, Mark broke free from the constable's grip and launched himself at his grandfather, punching him in the chest and stomach. "

You did it! You killed them!!! You killed them!!!" Mark's screams echoed through the chaos.

Kevin took the beating without raising a hand, while the constable eventually managed to pull Mark away. The young boy was wailing in grief and anger.

As the emergency workers placed two body bags into a van marked "Coroner," a crowd gathered behind a yellow barricade. Among them were a fifty-something couple, Laura and her partner, who held hands tightly. Behind them, stood a grim-faced man dressed in a conservative 2007 suit—Professor John Bentley. "This is too hard to take as their great-grandfather," he said, his voice heavy with emotion.

Laura turned to face him, her eyes questioning. "What did you say? You're not old enough to be their great grandfather."

"They must time travel to make things right," Professor Bentley explained.

Laura scoffed. "Of course, you could save two lives."

The Professor shook his head. "I can't stop deaths, I've tried. However, I might be able to stop a grandson hating his pop."

Laura and her partner exchanged confused looks, unable to comprehend what the Professor was saying. But they could see the pain etched on his face, and they knew, despite his absurd notion, that he was trying to make things right.

* * *

BENTLEY LIVING ROOM, 2007

Mark's tense body language and clenched jaw showed his bitterness as he spoke, his words laced with resentment and anger.

"He was arguing with my dad, and he was so caught up that he lost control and crashed," Mark's voice was cold, his words sharp like daggers. "If it wasn't for him, Mum and Dad would still be alive."

Gemma shook her head in disappointment, her expression conveying her disagreement. It was clear that she did not share Mark's view.

"That's pretty harsh, mate," Ben's voice was calm, but his eyebrows were raised in disbelief.

Mark's eyes narrowed and his body tensed even more at Ben's words. "You weren't there—and you don't have to live with him," he spat, his tone icy. Mark stormed out of the living room and headed towards the hall.

Gemma and Ben exchanged a look before following him, their footsteps echoing on the hardwood floors. The morning sunlight streamed through the large windows, casting warm golden rays into the room. The plush sofa and armchairs were arranged neatly around a coffee table, creating a cozy and inviting space. The walls were adorned with family photos and colorful paintings, giving the room a personal touch.

As Mark disappeared into the hallway, the tension in the living room dissipated, leaving behind a solemn atmosphere.

Gemma let out a heavy sigh and shook her head again, disappointed in Mark's bitterness and anger towards their grandfather. Ben walked over to one of the windows and gazed outside, his mind lost in thought. The peacefulness of the room was in stark contrast to the turmoil and conflict that Mark's words had brought. In this quiet living room, it was clear that words could hold so much power and emotion.

They could change the atmosphere of a room and the dynamics between people. And in this moment, Mark's words had left a lingering bitterness that hung in the air.

CHAPTER 4

THE BLUE ABYSS

SYDNEY HARBOUR - BEACH - MORNING

As the sun rose over the glistening waters of Sydney Harbour, Mark, Gemma, and Ben made their way to a secluded beach. They all sported flippers, face masks, and snorkels, while Ben carried a waterproof backpack. The sound of power boats and watercrafts zooming by could be heard in the distance.

Mark couldn't help but notice Ben's backpack and asked, "What's with the backpack?"

Ben replied, "Last time Dan was here, he got robbed while he was in the water. I'm not taking any chances."

Gemma added, "Ben's got my clothes too, Mark. And your phone."

Mark simply shrugged and shook his head in disbelief before diving into the crystal-clear water. Gemma and Ben followed suit, leaving behind any worries or doubts. As they explored the underwater world, colorful fish and coral reefs surrounded them. The sun's rays danced through the water, creating a mesmerizing effect. The sound of the waves lapping against the shore and the gentle breeze added to the tranquil atmosphere. Despite the beauty of their surroundings, the trio remained vigilant and cautious. They were not going to let anyone ruin their perfect morning at the beach.

Mark glides along the seabed, taking in the serenity of the ocean floor. He observes the small fish and sea flora that abound, mesmerized by the vibrant colors and delicate movements. In the distance, Ben and Gemma swim between rocks, following a large blue grouper until it darts into a crevice. Ben signals to go to the surface. Mark continues his journey along the ocean floor, marveling at the beauty around him. Suddenly, a four-meter-wide swirl of glowing blue water appeared in front of him. He shakes his head in disbelief and pauses, unsure of what he's seeing. With a sense of apprehension, he reaches out to touch the swirl, only to watch his hand disappear before his eyes. Mark is left in awe and disbelief.

Meanwhile, Ben and Gemma burst through the surface, ripping off their snorkels and gasping for air. Ben is ecstatic, exclaiming about the size of the grouper they just saw.

Gemma agrees, but her expression quickly turns to concern as she realizes Mark is nowhere to be seen. Frantically, they search for him, craning their heads in every direction.

Gemma calls out for Mark, her voice full of worry. They swim towards the center of the cove, hoping to find him there. Gemma signals downwards as they dive, determined to find their missing companion.

Ben and Gemma plunged into the depths of the Harbour; their bodies streamlined as they swam with purpose. Their eyes darted in every direction, scanning the murky waters with determination. Suddenly, Ben's hand shot out and he pointed towards a glowing swirl in the distance. Without hesitation, Gemma followed Ben's lead, her curiosity piqued by the strange phenomenon. She grabbed his arm and tugged, urging him to move faster.

But Ben was frozen in fear, his mind racing with thoughts of what could lie within the swirling waters. Gemma's eyes flicked back to Ben; her determination unwavering. She propelled herself forward with powerful kicks, her body slicing through the water.

With a deep breath, she lunged headlong into the swirling vortex, disappearing in an instant. For a moment, Ben hesitated, his heart pounding in his chest. But then, he closed his eyes and took a deep breath, steeling himself for what lay ahead. With a determined glint in his eye, he and Gemma glide into the unknown. As he entered the glowing swirl, Ben's surroundings blurred, and his senses were overwhelmed. The water felt thick and heavy against his skin, the light from the vortex casting an eerie glow.

And then, just like Gemma, he too disappeared into the blue abyss.

CHAPTER 5

BYGONE

The waves crashed against the rocky shore, the moon casting an eerie glow over the Harbour beach. Ben emerged from the depths, gasping for air as he broke through the surface. He looked around, disoriented and confused. Mark and Gemma, treading water nearby, remained calm.

"What the hell was that?" Ben yelled, his voice echoing through the night.

Mark swam over and grabbed Ben's shoulders. "Mate, you okay?"

Breathless, Ben replied, "Yeah. What just happened?"

Mark shook his head. "No idea. We swam into this blue swirly thing, and now we're here."

"But where? Where is *here?*" Ben asked, looking around at the unfamiliar landscape.

Gemma joined them, her voice filled with disbelief. "What the fu—? How can it be night?"

The trio heard the rising chug-chug of a circa 1940 ferry engine. They were bewildered, unable to understand how they had ended up in a different time and place. The darkness enveloped them, the only source of light coming from the moon above. The sound of the waves and the distant engine filled the air, creating a strong sense of setting.

Ben, Mark, and Gemma were each trying to make sense of their surroundings. As they looked around, they noticed small but impactful details—the rough texture of the rocks, the salty smell of the sea, and the cold water against their skin. However, their focus remained on the mysterious events that had brought them here, and they couldn't help but wonder what would happen next. The trio's confusion and disbelief were noticeable, as they tried to make sense of their situation. This was just the beginning of their journey, and they could never have imagined the events that would unfold in the coming days. The night was still young, and Ben, Mark, and Gemma had no idea what awaited them in this strange new world.

A faded, weathered 1940s Ferry emerges from behind the shadowy headland of the beach, slowly revealing itself to the few passengers on board. The engines' deafening roar fades into the background, replaced by a faint ringing of a bell.

Mark, Gemma, and Ben appear from the water, removing their masks and snorkels as they trudge onto the shore. The sand is littered with looming rocks, casting an eerie atmosphere.

"I've got all our stuff," Ben boasts, smirking as he pulls a towel and clothes from his bag.

Mark's expression turns sour as he storms off. "I'm going back to the car," his voice echoes from a distance.

Gemma follows, her bikini top and board shorts still damp from their snorkeling adventure. Ben rummages through his backpack and pulls out a wrinkled T-shirt.

As they appeared from the thick scrub, Gemma and Ben were greeted by the cool night air. Gemma shivered, pulling her white fitted top tighter around her. She glanced down at her phone, then looked at Ben, who had a confused expression on his face. He too was staring at his phone, which showed no signal. They joined Mark, who was already in the clearing, his body language portraying annoyance and disillusionment.

His hands were flailing in the air as he exclaimed, "No car! There's no friggin' car!"

Ben shook his head, "I told you we shouldn't trust those shitheads!"

Mark spun around in frustration, taking in their surroundings. Gemma and Ben followed his gaze, their eyes scanning the roadside scrub. The setting sun had now given way to the darkness of the night.

"This can't be right. We must have taken the wrong path," Ben spoke, the disbelief clear in his voice.

Mark was quick to refute, "There's only one path from the beach to the parking lot. And I've walked it a hundred times."

Gemma looked around, trying to make sense of their situation, "So, no car, no parking lot. Are we in the *Twilight Zone?*"

Ben's mind was already working on a solution. "We should call the cops."

Mark had a different idea. "I'm pretty sure there's a bus stop nearby. We can take a bus back to the city." He pointed to his right, and the trio followed his directions, their feet crunching on the dry leaves and twigs.

Gemma's heart raced as she took in the eerie surroundings. The darkness seemed to amplify every sound and movement, making her more and more anxious. As they walked, Ben couldn't help but think about the events of the day. The bright and sunny day had suddenly turned into the dark and cold night. And now, they were stranded in the middle of nowhere with no car in sight. He couldn't help but feel like something was not right. As they finally reached the bus stop, Ben pushed those thoughts aside. They needed to focus on finding a way back home. And as they waited for the bus, Gemma couldn't help but wonder if they had stumbled into some kind of alternate reality, where nothing was as it seemed, and everything was a little off.

Mark, Gemma, and Ben stood on the dark street, surrounded by Edwardian houses. They were confused, their eyes darting around in search of any sign of direction. As they made their way towards what they thought was a bus stop, a sudden sound caught their attention. It was the unfamiliar ring of a 1940's tram bell. Their mouths dropped open in surprise as they watched the Bondi Tram approaching them.

The tram screeched to a stop in the middle of the road, its wheels grinding against the pavement. The trio could do nothing but stand there, their eyes wide with shock. They were unsure of what to do next.

Suddenly, the tram driver poked his head out of the window and called out to them. "Oi! You lot getting on?" he yelled.

Gemma's eyes widened even further, her mind reeling at the bizarre situation they were in. "This is definitely like something out of the *Twilight Zone*," she muttered, shaking her head in disbelief. Without a word, Gemma made her way towards the tram's door. Mark and Ben followed her uncertainly, their eyes still glued to the strange vehicle in front of them.

Mark, Gemma and Ben sat in the well-used wood and leather vehicle, the only passengers on board. The Conductor sat close by head down and forlorn, lost in his own thoughts.

Gemma at once reached out and gently patted his arm, showing her concern, "Excuse me, sir. Are you okay?" Gemma asked, her voice laced with empathy.

The Conductor didn't respond, his eyes fixed straight ahead, lost in a trance-like state.

"Excuse me!" Gemma raised her voice, trying to break through to the Conductor.

Startled, the Conductor snapped back to reality, "Sorry. Had some bad news today. I was a million miles away," he explained with a heavy sigh.

"What happened?" Gemma inquired; her eyes filled with genuine concern.

The Conductor shifted in his seat, clearly uncomfortable. "It's just my brother," he finally confessed.

"What about your brother?" Gemma probed further, wanting to understand.

Taking a deep breath, the Conductor revealed, "The war office told me today that...he died—died in the war."

The trio was moved by his heartbreaking revelation. "I'm so sorry for your loss," Gemma offered sympathetically, her hand still resting on the Conductor's arm. "Was he stationed in Iraq?"

"No, New Guinea. He was missing in action, but they found his body and let the family know this morning," the Conductor replied, his voice heavy with sorrow.

Ben, who had been quietly observing the interaction, spoke up. "Peace-keeping troops, I bet. Poor dude. I feel sorry for him." The trio fell into a somber silence, reflecting on the Conductor's loss.

Slowly, the Conductor rose from his seat and made his way past them to the front of the tram.

"Don't worry about paying. There's no inspector tonight. It's on me," he said, leaving the trio feeling melancholy and reflective as they gazed out into the darkness outside.

The wood and leather vehicle creaked as it moved along the tracks, the only sound breaking the solemn atmosphere. The dim lighting inside the tram cast a melancholic glow, and the trio couldn't help but feel a sense of heaviness in the air. Amidst the sorrow and grief, there was a sense of camaraderie and understanding between the passengers and the Conductor. In that moment, they were all connected by the shared human experience of loss and grief. It was a powerful reminder that even in the darkest of times, there is still light and hope to be found.

The Bondi tram comes to a halt, shaking its passengers as it screeches to a stop. Mark, Gemma, and Ben hop off, their eyes wide with disbelief as they take in their surroundings.

The bell rings, signaling their departure as the tram disappears into the darkness.

Mark looks around, his mouth agape, and exclaims, "What the hell?"

Gemma's gaze follows his and she sees the buildings along Campbell Parade, a long street that runs along Bondi Beach. Most of the buildings are either dark or dimly lit.

"What's going on with the barbed wire?" Gemma asks, her voice filled with confusion.

Ben's eyes widen in shock as he takes in the sight before him. "Holy shit! Where are we?"

Mark's incredulous gaze falls upon a gun turret and a line of parked 1930s cars.

"Mate, this is weird. Look at this," he says, pointing at the cars.

"These belong in a museum," Gemma's eyebrows furrow in confusion.

"What the hell is going on?" Mark shakes his head and says, "If I didn't know any better, I'd say we were in Bondi sixty years ago."

Ben slaps himself and rubs his eyes in disbelief. "That can't be. We must be dreaming."

"It's too real," Mark replies, his voice filled with conviction.

Gemma suggests, "Something must have happened to us when we swam into that blue swirl. Check your mobile, Ben."

Ben reaches into his bag and pulls out his mobile phone. He tries to make a call, but there is no signal. "Nup, still nothing. What now?"

Mark's eyes light up as he says, "This is too freaky. But you know what? I feel like a beer."

"Me too!" Ben agrees. "After all, we are still in Bondi. Let's find a pub."

Gemma looks at them, her dismay clear on her face. "We're in the *Twilight Zone*, and you guys are going drinking?"

Mark shrugs. "Absolutely!"

Gemma shakes her head in disbelief, unsure of what to make of their situation.

Mark and Ben strolled up the grassy knoll towards the 1940's décor Hotel Bondi. Gemma hesitated, her heart racing as she watched them leave her behind.

"Don't leave me here. Don't you dare leave me!" she pleaded, her voice trembling with fear.

Ben looked back at her with a smirk. "Maybe your gramps slipped something into our iced coffees and we're just tripping," he joked, trying to ease the tension.

A prim mother passed by with her impossibly neat seven-year-old son and nine-year-old daughter. The daughter pointed towards Mark, Ben, and Gemma; her eyes wide with curiosity. "Mum, look at those people dressed in funny clothes," she said. The mother's face twisted in disapproval.

"Stay close, Nancy. They might be Nazis," she warned, her eyes narrowing at Gemma. "That girl looks like a lady of the night! My goodness!"

Gemma shot the prim mother a dirty look and stuck her tongue out after they passed by. She couldn't believe the judgmental attitude of some people.

As Mark, Gemma, and Ben made their way along Campbell Parade, they couldn't help but notice the stares from pedestrians passing by. The pedestrians gawked back at them; their curiosity evident. Suddenly, two soldiers yelled at the trio from a passing vehicle.

"Go back to the Cross, you bloody Bohemians!" one of them shouted.

The other one added in a sleazy tone, "Nice boobs, darlin'!"

Gemma felt self-conscious and immediately covered her top with crossed arms. She couldn't believe the creepy men. She gazed at the streetlights, trying to distract herself from the situation. "I'm in a nightmare. These dim lights don't help," she mumbled, her voice filled with frustration.

Ben shook his head in disbelief. "How do these people even drive around?" he wondered aloud.

Mark scoffed. "These bulbs must produce all of two and a half watts!" he exclaimed, shaking his head in disapproval. He walked over to one of the streetlight poles and touched it, inspecting the light. Gemma and Ben followed suit; their eyes fixated on the weak light bulbs.

The dim lighting added to the eerie atmosphere, making Gemma feel even more uneasy. She couldn't wait to leave this strange, old-fashioned world behind.

CHAPTER 6

BONDI?

Mark, Gemma and Ben move cautiously into the Hotel Bondi, their heads held low as they soak in the atmosphere. The sound of laughter and chatter fills the air as they enter the bar, their eyes scanning the room. Soldiers, dressed in their uniforms, occupy most of the seats, their presence commanding attention. The trio takes in the 1940's themed bar, with its wooden and chrome furnishings, giving off a sense of nostalgia.

As they make their way through the crowd, a hush falls over the bar, all eyes turning towards them. Gemma feels a wave of embarrassment wash over her as she notices the men ogling her. She crosses her arms, trying to hide her discomfort.

Taking in the scene, Ben can't help but exclaim in surprise, "What the—!"

Mark, on the other hand, can't believe what he's seeing. "This ain't the Hotel Bondi I remember," he mutters in disbelief.

One soldier, with a beer in hand, walks by Gemma, his gaze lingering on her top. "Look at the tits on that!" he comments, causing Gemma to roll her eyes in annoyance.

"You've never seen breasts before, asshole?" she retorts, unimpressed by the soldier's crude comment.

But he doesn't back down, replying with a sleazy grin, "Not like yours, darl'."

Mark steps in, trying to diffuse the situation. "Give her a break, mate," he says, trying to reason with the soldier.

But before things can escalate further, an old bar worker approaches Gemma, collecting glasses as he speaks. "Sorry love, you have to cover them up," he says apologetically.

Gemma's anger and discomfort only intensify as she sneers at the worker and Ben quickly comes to her rescue, placing his jacket over her shoulders. She buttons it up, feeling the weight of the crowd's stares as the trio continues to make their way through the bar.

Suddenly, Ben's phone interrupts the tension, playing Nirvana's 'Smells Like Teen Spirit.' He quickly silences it, apologizing for the interruption. "Oops, my alarm," he says with a hesitant smile. "It's just Nirvana."

The soldiers, who were ready to pounce on the trio for their perceived intrusion, now relax upon hearing the tune.

"Are you blokes bible bashers?" one of them jokes.

"Don't come in here to preach on us!" adds another, his tone lightening.

Mark, sensing the change in atmosphere, decides to play along. He throws his arms in the air, acting crazy as he shouts, "Ah, hell no! We're here to get fuckin' pissed!" The crowd cheers, accepting their explanation, and the bar noise swells once again.

People return to their conversations and drinks, the trio now blending in with the rest of the crowd. As they make their way to the bar, they pass two sailors, who can't help but make snarky comments, "These ladies look like they were dropped off a U-boat," one of them jokes, earning a laugh from his companion.

The other sailor then turns his attention to Ben's low-rider jeans and exposed boxers. "Oi, what's holding them pants up?" he asks, his own tight white bell bottoms contrasting with Ben's fashion sense.

Ben is quick to defend himself, "Really? Have you ever heard of a mirror?"

The sailor, offended by the comment, moves to grab Ben, but his friend holds him back, warning him about the Provos outside.

The trio finally reaches the bar, and one of the soldiers addresses Gemma, "We don't normally allow Sheila's in this bar," he says, "but we'll make an exception for you."

Gemma responds with a deadpan expression, "Wow, thanks, I'm flattered."

The soldier, with a gaunt appearance and a closed-mouth grin, can't help but admire Gemma's figure and her shiny top. He leans in closer and remarks, "Your top sparkles, like my tooth." With a proud smile, he reveals a single gold tooth among his rotten dentures. Gemma waves her hand in front of her nose, indicating his bad breath.

Gemma, Mark, and Ben push their way through the crowded bar, their eyes scanning the dimly lit room for a place to sit.

The sound of glasses clinking, and laughter fills the air as they make their way towards the bar. A man dressed in a white shirt and black vest stands behind the bar, wiping a glass with a cloth. Ben steps up to the bar and confidently orders three schooners of 'Cold.'

"Thanks mate," Ben says, flashing a charming smile.

"They're all cold," the barman replies, his tone slightly annoyed.

"Whatever," Ben shrugs, reaching into his pocket for some money.

"That'll be two bob," the barman says, holding out his hand. Ben eagerly hands over a ten-dollar bill, feeling satisfied with his choice of bar.

But the barman's reaction surprises him. "Crickey! What's this stuff?" the barman exclaims, holding up the colorful bill to examine it.

Mark and Gemma exchange a confused look as a sharply dressed man named Cedric slides up next to them, his posture exuding confidence and a hint of flamboyance. "Can I offer to buy you good people a drink?" Cedric says, his voice pompous and slightly camp.

The trio is taken aback by Cedric's approach. Gemma leans into whisper to Ben. "Oh. My. God. You're getting cruised!" she giggles.

Ben looks at her with confusion, not understanding what she means.

"I think he's gay," Gemma continues, trying to contain her laughter. But before they can react, Cedric is standing next to them, overhearing their conversation.

"Thanks a lot," Ben says awkwardly, feeling uncomfortable under Cedric's gaze. "And are you?"

Cedric smiles and raises his shoulder, looking at Gemma.

"Well, how perceptive, pretty lady," he says, his tone flirtatious. "Most people say I'm a jolly chap."

Ben's face turns red withembarrassment as Mark steps in to clarify. "Ben, are you stupid? Jolly chaps like Cedric are gay. Carpet munchers are lesbos," Mark says, trying to educate Ben on different terms.

Cedric looks at them with amusement, not understanding the term "lesbo." "I'm a gay man, but what is this 'lesbo' you speak of?" he asks, genuinely curious.

Gemma steps in to change the subject, eager to tell Cedric about their eventful night, "Cedric, it's wonderful to meet you. You won't believe what a night we've had," she says, making small talk.

"Oh, do tell, lovely! Do tell!" Cedric exclaims, his attention fully on Gemma.

Meanwhile, a soldier in the background listens in on their conversation, intrigued by their lively exchange. Soldier Boyd, an ocker and rough man, calls out to Cedric with a boorish ocker voice, "Oi! Right! They got you there, Ceddy boy!"

Cedric raises his eyebrows indignantly and retorts in a low voice, "You wish!" He pauses, "Well, you guessed my little secret. You're so perceptive, honey!" as he touches Ben's arm. Cedric retreats and raises his hand in acknowledgement before paying the barman and grabbing their beers. They all sit at the bar, taking in their surroundings. Mark introduces himself, Ben, and Gemma to Cedric. As they shake hands, Cedric asks what brings them to this place.

Ben responds with a dismissive, "Don't ask," implying that they are not from around here.

Cedric notices Gemma's revealing outfit and offers her fashion advice. He warns her to cover up or else she will be the target of unwanted attention from the three oddball soldiers ogling her. Gemma agrees and asks Cedric for the date. Cedric at once responds with May 30th. However, Mark clarifies that they are not asking for the day, but for the year.

Cedric hands Ben a newspaper, and as they read the date, they are shocked to realize that they have traveled back in time to 1942!

Amid their shock, Ben spits his beer on Cedric's suit, apologizing quickly.

Gemma points out the obvious changes in the surroundings—the cars, buildings, and people. She realizes that they have somehow traveled back in time and urges the group to stay calm and not reveal their true identities. Ben recalls a book he read about the dangers of altering the past, using the example of Ashton Kutcher in *The Butterfly Effect*. Mark is confused, but Ben warns them not to make any changes that could have negative consequences in the future.

Mark, slurring his words, half-shouts, "I'm legless every Friday night!"

Ben just rolled his eyes at his mate's drunken antics. Gemma, on the other hand, shot Mark a sharp glare, her frustration clear.

In the background, a large, buttoned-down U.S. Marine stood, his imposing figure casting a shadow over the group. The Marine casually placed a hand on Ben's shoulder, causing him to jump in surprise.

"I just wanted to ask you something," the Marine said with a hint of caution in his voice.

Ben gulped nervously, unsure of what to expect. "Yes?" he replied cautiously.

The Marine's gaze drifted down to Ben's feet, which were sporting a new pair of sneakers.

"Where did you get those shoes?" the Marine asked, his curiosity piqued.

Ben breathed a sigh of relief, glad that the Marine's attention was on his footwear and not on Mark's drunken state. "At Nike, in Bondi Junction," he answered, feeling a sense of pride in his new purchase.

The Marine raised an eyebrow, "Nike sounds Japanese. Are you sure you guys are from around here?"

Mark scoffed, "Yeah, we've lived on Lamrock Avenue our whole lives."

The Marine's offer caught Ben off guard as he eyed the Marine's worn sneakers. "Interested in swapping?" he asked, gesturing to Ben's shoes.

Ben shook his head. "Not really, but we'd consider it if you threw in some cash."

The Marine's frown deepened as he reached into his pocket and pulled out three notes. "They're pretty neat," he admitted, handing them over to Ben.

Ben turned to Gemma, whispering, "Is that a lot?"

Gemma couldn't help but chuckle. "In 1942, you could practically buy a house with that."

Ben's eyes widened. "Okay. Three quid!"

The Marine nodded. "You got yourself a deal." As he handed over the money, his expression turned serious. "I may sound harsh, but in the Marines, we value function over fashion."

Ben nodded, a newfound respect for the Marine's practicality. "I'll keep that in mind," he replied, feeling a little embarrassed by his earlier boast about his sneakers.

The group exchanged glances, each of them taken aback by Ben's unexpected knowledge of footwear.

"Hey, chicks dig Italian high heels. I dig Nike," Ben defended himself, trying to save face.

The Marine chuckled. "Tell you what, these might sound Japanese, but they're worth more than two quid." He handed over one more note, making it a total of three. As the Marine walked away, Ben couldn't help but feel a sense of pride in his new sneakers and a newfound appreciation for the Marine's practicality.

Mark, Gemma, and Ben stroll into the Lounge, exuding an air of relaxation and inebriation. They saunter past a bustling crowd that includes several women and a few soldiers sporting Ben's personal items—his ID bracelet, watch, and of course, his shoes. The trio smirks, clearly pleased with their purchases.

"Nice move, Ben," Mark remarks, counting the money in his hands.

As they make their way through the room, they catch the attention of two matrons in fancy hats who stare at Gemma's outfit with disapproval. A haughty woman, draped in a fox stole, sneers at Gemma, commenting, "My, my, what do those street ladies wear these days?"

Gemma, unbothered, retorts, "At least I'm not parading around with a butchered animal on my neck."

The haughty woman scoffs, "Well, that lady of the night is so common."

Mark and Ben head to the men's restroom, leaving Gemma to wait outside. As Ben's jacket slips open, a group of drunken sailors' eye Gemma up and down, making lewd comments. Gemma ignores their advances, trying to remain calm and unbothered.

"So, love, how much for a quickie?" one of them slurred.

Gemma, infuriated, snaps back, "Look, I am not a lady of the night. Just leave me alone."

But the sailors continue to make crude offers, with one even grabbing her. Gemma retreats, only to be confronted by more sailors. She freezes, fear creeping in.

Suddenly, a voice cuts through the chaos, "Oi! Leave her alone!" It's Mark, who has come out of the restroom with Ben.

The sailors turn to face Mark, but he stands his ground, his eyes blazing with anger. Ben stands behind him, nervously shuffling his feet.

"We're just having a bit of fun with a young lass," one of the sailor's slurs, trying to brush it off.

"That's my sister," Mark growls, his tone leaving no room for argument. "Take your fun somewhere else, dude."

"Yeah, that's his sister!" Ben chimes in, trying to sound tough.

Mark and Ben quickly grab Gemma and push past the sailors, heading for the exit. One of the sailors tries to take a swing at Mark, but misses and falls onto a drinker, spilling his beer. A prim and proper woman lets out a high-pitched shriek as the beer splashes onto her. The drinker shoves Mark, and during the chaos, one of the sailors punches him in the jaw. Another sailor jumps on Ben, putting him in a head-lock. Gemma, not one to back down, jumps on the sailor's back and uses her feet to knock two others over. She quickly gets up and continues to fight, while Mark and Ben defend themselves as well.

The scene quickly escalates into a full-blown barroom brawl, with glasses shattering and fists flying. The chaos catches the attention of four military police officers, who rush in with whistles blowing, trying to restore order. The lounge is left in disarray, with broken glasses and overturned tables. The trio, now battered and bruised, stands in the middle of the chaos, panting and trying to catch their breath. But they can't help but grin, knowing they have made quite an impact on the otherwise peaceful evening.

Outside the pub, Ben, Gemma, and Mark stood handcuffed and down-trodden next to a vintage Paddy Wagon while a perplexed Provo scrutinized their licenses. The trio's birth year, 1987, caught Provo Whitehead's attention, and he questioned how they were able to obtain such high quality photos. Provo Sengos, equally bewildered, examined the licenses, noting their unusual material.

Mark clarified that they were authentic. Impressed, Provo Sengos admitted he wouldn't mind having one himself.

Provo Whitehead, on the other hand, was more concerned with why the three of them weren't enlisted in the military. He warned that they had no authority and would have to hand them over to the police.

Without hesitation, the Provos forcefully shoved the trio into the back of the paddy wagon and drove off at speed.

CHAPTER 7

CAPTIVITY

Gemma, Mark, and Ben sat on the cold, hard floor of the Bondi Police Station cell. They looked defeated, their shoulders slumped, and their eyes filled with worry. Police Constables Nicholas and Mitchell stood outside the cell, their watchful eyes scanning the room.

"We usually separate the men and women, but tonight's been crazy. No room," Constable Nicholas said, his voice tired and his face lined with exhaustion.

Mark's voice trembled as he spoke up, "So, you're going to let us go? We didn't start the fight."

Nicholas shook his head. "No, we need to hold you for our enquiries. We checked the address you gave us, and the people there have never heard of you."

Constable Mitchell chimed in, a hint of disbelief in his voice, "Are you guys from the movies or something? This radio thing looks like it belongs to Buck Rogers!"

Constable Nicholas picked up Ben's mobile phone and examined it closely, his fingers tapping on the keypad. "This has got us stumped. A walkie-talkie with pictures? My brother in Army Intelligence had no idea these existed."

Mark's face fell, and he looked at Ben with worry. "Will they let us go if we check out okay?"

Constable Nicholas shook his head. "No, Army Intelligence will want to speak to you both tomorrow."

He left, leaving the trio alone in the cell. They sat on their bare, uncomfortable beds, the coldness of the room seeping into their bones.

Mark spoke up again, his voice filled with fear, "They'll put us in the loony bin!"

Mark and Ben lay down on their backs, staring up at the plain ceiling. The reality of their situation is sinking in.

* * *

The next day, Bondi Police Station was bustling with activity as the morning shift began. Constables Pankhurst and Gooch entered, ready to start their day. They greeted each other with a nod and a brief exchange of words, while ConstablesNicholas and Mitchell were busy scribbling notes behind the front desk.

"How's it been?" Constable Pankhurst asked, taking a sip of his steaming cup of coffee.

"The usual," replied Constable Nicholas with a hint of annoyance. "Drunkards and crazies causing trouble."

Constable Pankhurst chuckled, knowing all too well the kind of characters that frequented the police station. "So, who are we releasing this morning?" he asked, already anticipating the answer.

"Those two blokes in Cell 1," Constable Nicholas answered, gesturing towards the cells, "They've had a wild night and are ready to go home. But Cell 2 is a different story. Waiting for Army Intelligence. We have to keep them locked up."

Constable Pankhurst nodded, understanding the seriousness of the situation. "Alright Nicho, I'll take care of it. You go and have some fun," he said with a wink.

With that, Constables Nicholas and Mitchell grabbed their work bags and left, leaving the station in the capable hands of Constable Pankhurst and Gooch. The sound of their footsteps echoed in the otherwise quiet station, a reminder of the never-ending cycle of work and duty.

Police Constable Pankhurst sat behind the desk, shuffling through a stack of paperwork. The incessant ringing of the phone disrupted the quiet of the station, and he answered it with a sigh. Constable Gooch stood by his side, watching as his colleague took the call.

"So, who's going?" Constable Gooch inquired, his gaze shifting between the paperwork and the phone call.

Constable Pankhurst pressed the phone to his ear, his face betraying no emotion. "No worries, I'll wait outside," he said calmly into the receiver. With a brief pause, he placed his hand over the mouthpiece and turned to Constable Gooch, "Number 2 cell can go," he said, his voice low and firm.

In the cell area of the police station, Constable Gooch entered with purpose. He glanced up at the sign that read, "Cells" and took in the scene before him. Mark, Gemma, and Ben were still asleep, their forms huddled together on the hard benches. Constable Gooch unlocked the cell nd stepped inside, his footsteps echoing against the cold, bare walls.

"Wakey, wakey!" he called out, his voice booming in the small space. "You lot can go."

Ben stirred from his slumber, rubbing his eyes and stretching his sore limbs. "But the other bloke said..." he began to protest, but Gemma quickly silenced him with a sharp smack to his leg. "He said we could go, too," Ben finished, now more quietly.

With a knowing look, Constable Gooch nodded and gestured for them to follow him out of the cell. As they made their way back to the main desk, Ben couldn't help but feel a sense of relief wash over him. He was grateful for the kind-hearted policemen who showed them mercy and allowed them to go free.

Outside, a paddy wagon squeals to a stop, Constable Pankhurst springs into action, racing to the front of the vehicle. Two prisoners, wild and unruly, put up a fierce fight as they are dragged towards the station. Constable Pankhurst springs into action, working tirelessly to bring the situation under control.

Inside the police station, Mark, Ben, and Gemma nervously stand before the front desk, with Constable Gooch standing beside them. Without a word, Constable Gooch hands them a bag for their personal belongings. The trio quickly pack their backpacks, grab their licenses, iPods, wallets, and phones before scurrying to hide behind the door. In the chaos, Constable Pankhurst struggles with the prisoners as they are dragged inside.

Sensing an opportunity, Mark, Ben, and Gemma make a break for it, darting out of the station as Constable Pankhurst is occupied. Outside, Constable Gooch catches up to the trio, his stern voice cutting through the air, "No more drinking, you lot!"

Mark quickly assures him that they are sober and on the straight and narrow.

The three friends pick up their pace, breaking into a run as they round the corner. The streets of Bondi are alive with the sights and sounds of bustling city life. The sun beats down on the pavement as the trio makes their escape, their hearts racing with adrenaline. With each step, they leave their troubles behind, determined to start anew in 1940s Bondi.

As Mark, Gemma, and Ben made their way down the bustling street, the sound of their feet pounding against the pavement echoed through the air. They moved with a sense of urgency, their steps quick and determined.

Gemma suddenly came to a halt, her eyes fixed on a large department store with the words "Gowings" emblazoned on its front.

Without a word, she made her way inside, the boys following closely behind. The trio's sudden appearance in the store caused a few curious glances from the other shoppers, but they paid them no mind. They had a mission to complete, and time was of the essence.

As they arrived at the beach, Gemma's conservative dress and pumps swayed gracefully in the ocean breeze. Mark, in his open shirt and baggy wool pants, casually took a seat on the promenade next to Ben, who looked sharp in his suit and fedora, with a backpack slung over his shoulder. They took in the sight before them—barbed wire and barriers, a stark reminder of the uncertain times they lived in.

"It makes you realize how lucky we were in our own time," Ben commented, his tone reflecting a mix of nostalgia and relief.

Mark nodded in agreement. "Yep, there might be terrorism, but it's not on our doorstep yet."

Gemma fidgeted with her dress, clearly uncomfortable in her formal attire.

Mark, noticing her discomfort, joked, "Don't know if I like this. You'd rather have horny soldiers groping you?"

Gemma playfully pushed him away. "No way," she firmly stated, shaking her head.

Ben, always the fashion-forward one, chimed in, "A great time for sharp-dressed men."

Gemma couldn't help but push him again, teasing, "You're such a 'fashionista'. You know, grandpa was stationed at Garden Island in 1942."

"That's what he said yesterday." Ben corrected himself, momentarily confused, "I mean sixty years from now."

"We know what you mean," Mark reassured him.

"When did he say he was bashed?" Gemma asked, suddenly realizing the significance of the date.

"May 31st," Mark replied. "He told us a hundred times."

"That's today!" Gemma exclaimed, a sense of destiny washing over her. "Freaky that we should arrive the day before." She paused, pondering their situation. "It's got to be our destiny. I think we should contact him."

Mark, however, was adamant. "Remember what they said, don't do anything to change the past."

Gemma raised an eyebrow, questioning the mysterious "they" that Mark referred to.

"First of all, I don't know who 'they' are that you're talking about," she said matter-of-factly, "And secondly, Gran and Pop are our age. How many people get to see their grandparents, young? We won't tell them who we are."

Mark hesitated, then reluctantly agreed. "Oh, okay. But I'm only going to see Gran. Couldn't care less about Pop." Gemma gave him a look, silently questioning his lack of interest in their grandfather.

But Ben intervened, reminding them of the three main time travel rules. "One, don't kill anyone. Two, don't give out info. And Three, don't step on anything."

Gemma couldn't help but ask, "Again, who made those rules?"

Ben shrugged, "Does it really matter? It's still good advice, okay?" All three nodded in agreement, their excitement and curiosity palpable. This was the opportunity of a lifetime, and they were determined not to mess it up.

In a bustling Bondi Milk Bar, Gemma stands at the counter with Ben and Mark. She hesitantly picks up the phone, feeling the intense gaze of the middle-aged Milk Bar Owner upon her. Mark watches in dismay as Gemma dials the number with trembling fingers.

"It's like texting for dummies," Mark remarks, glancing at Ben.

"Yeah, I bet you couldn't have charmed him into a free call," Ben retorts, clutching his chest in mock pain.

Gemma interrupts their banter, "Hello, operator? Could you connect me with Kevin Bentley in Woolloomooloo?" The voice on the other end connects Gemma to a ringing phone.

A woman, Alice, answers.

"Hello?" Alice's voice crackles through the receiver.

Gemma's heart races as she asks, "Is Kevin Bentley there?"

"No, he's out. Can I take a message?" Alice replies.

With quick thinking, Gemma responds, "This is Marie, a friend of his. Will Kevin be home tonight?"

"Marie? He's never mentioned you. Aren't you coming to the party then?" Alice questions.

Gemma is momentarily taken aback, but quickly recovers, "Of course! We'll be there."

"Well, I'll see you tonight," Alice says before hanging up.

Gemma hangs up the phone, her mind racing. She turns to the boys, excitement in her eyes. "He's having a party! This is our perfect chance to see him. We can say we came with a friend."

Mark offers a glimmer of hope, "He might not even be at the party after the mugging. Maybe he's in the hospital."

"Then we'll go to the hospital," Gemma declares determinedly.

Curiosity strikes Mark. "Who did you speak to?"

Gemma hesitates, then realization dawns on her. "She sounded middle-aged."

She and Mark exchange shocked looks.

"You spoke to our great-grandmother. She died twenty years before we were born!" Mark exclaims in disbelief.

The trio excitedly leave the milk bar, with Ben pulling out a skateboard from his backpack.

Gemma grabs it with a grin. "Cool!"

As they leave, the Milk Bar Owner watches Gemma's swaying hips, a smirk on his face.

"Come back anytime," he calls after them, his eyes fixed on Gemma's backside.

CHAPTER 8

RECON

As the Japanese "A Class" submarine silently prowled the waters twelve kilometers north-east of Sydney's northern beaches, a small plane was launched from its deck. The lone pilot, dressed in a Japanese uniform, expertly controlled the toy-like aircraft. Its sleek design and tiny rising sun symbol on the tail gave a hint of its origin. With graceful movements, it ascended into the sky, disappearing into the clouds.

The pilot's expression showed his determination to complete his mission. The distant sound of the ocean and the occasional seagull's cry created a serene atmosphere, in stark contrast to the tension on the submarine. The crew watched with bated breath, waiting for the pilot's return. Two more ominous "A Class" Submarines are close by.

As the plane disappeared from sight, the captain's voice broke the silence. "We must not fail," he said sternly, his eyes fixed on the Sydney shoreline. The crew knew the importance of their mission and the risks involved. They could only hope for a successful outcome as they continued their journey towards their target.

The plane's engines hummed as it soared at 5000 feet above Manly Beach in Sydney, the turquoise waters glistening below. The Japanese Pilot's sharp gaze scanned the beach, shops, and bustling Harbour, his hands steady on the controls. Despite his mission, he marveled at the bustling city below, the vibrant colors and sounds filling his senses.

* * *

Simon, a twelve-year-old boy, sat perched atop the rooftop deck of the Manly Stein Hotel. He peered through his binoculars, tracking the movements of the small Japanese recon plane in the sky. His heart raced as he struggled to make sense of what he was seeing. He rubbed his eyes, hoping it was just a figment of his imagination. But as he flicked through the pages of a nearby War Planes book, the truth became clear.

"Crikey!" he exclaimed; his voice filled with disbelief. "It's a bloody Jap recon plane."

Without hesitation, Simon leapt to his feet, nearly losing his balance in the process. He sprinted towards the door, shouting for his dad at the top of his lungs, "Dad! Dad!"

He bounded down two flights of stairs, his heart pounding in his chest. Finally, he reached his father, who was serving a beer to a sailor on leave at the bar.

"Dad, I know this sounds crazy, but I just saw a Jap recon plane flying west towards the Bridge!"

The sailor chuckled, casting a sceptical glance at Ron. "Has the kid been sneaking sips of that Yank Lager on the roof, Ron?"

Ron shook his head, a serious look on his face. "No, he hates the taste of beer."

The sailor shrugged, taking a sip from his glass. "Well, that makes two of us with that Yankee shit."

Simon's excitement quickly turned to disappointment as his father sternly addressed him. "Simon, you need to control that wild imagination of yours. People won't believe you when you tell them something important. Now go do your homework."

Deflated, Simon hung his head and slowly shuffled away. "But Dad—"

Ron glared at him, cutting him off.

With a heavy heart, Simon left the bar, feeling defeated and misunderstood.

* * *

As the Japanese plane soared above Sydney Harbour, the pilot's eyes fixated on the iconic Sydney Harbour Bridge below. With a calm and collected demeanor, he spoke into his radio, relaying his position and plans. The radio crackled to life, a voice responding in Japanese. The pilot listened intently; his gaze still focused on the bustling harbor below.

He confirmed his altitude and his route, mentioning a specific destination before returning to base. The voice on the radio asked a question, and the pilot's affirmative response was filled with a sense of purpose. He had seen the enemy's ships, including a powerful US Destroyer stationed at Garden Island Base. With efficiency and precision, he promised to provide a diagram of their positions on his return flight.

With his mission accomplished, the pilot ended the call and maneuvered his plane towards Drummoyne. The roar of the engine filled his ears as he banked steeply, his mind already planning his next move. The cool air rushed past him, carrying with it the scent of saltwater and the sound of distant voices. As the plane glided over the bustling city, the pilot's focus remained unbroken, determined to complete his mission.

* * *

The tram-stop on Campbell Parade in 1942 was bustling with activity. Mark and Ben were sitting on the bench, waiting for their tram. Gemma was whizzing around them on her skateboard.

Suddenly, a truck full of U.S. Marines pulled up and Duane, a stern-jawed marine in his twenties, jumped out. He couldn't help but whistle at Gemma, who smiled in response. As he bent down to take a closer look at her board, he couldn't help but sneak a glance at her body. Gemma, clearly proud of her skateboard, boasted that it was an Aussie invention, and that Americans weren't the only innovators.

Duane was impressed by her sassy attitude and intelligence. Interrupting her, he exclaimed, "Oooh—sassy and intelligent. I like this rolling board."

Gemma quickly corrected him, "Skateboard. It's called a skateboard."

Ben introduced himself and Mark, and Duane shook their hands. He then made an offer—if they let him ride their skateboard, he would arrange for them to visit the *U.S.S. Chicago*. Excited, the trio happily agreed. Gemma asked Duane if he was stationed at Garden Island, and he confirmed this.

Mark chimed in, "That's next to Pop's place."

Gemma handed over their skateboard to Duane and jumped into the truck. He wasted no time putting the skateboard on the ground and attempting to ride it, but he ended up tumbling over. One of the marines joked, "You'll be an expert in seven years, Duane."

Mark reassured him, "No worries. We'll show you how at the base."

Another marine chimed in, "Just four hundred and sixty easy lessons." Duane laughed good-naturedly.

As the truck roars down the road, Duane springs onto the back, his heart racing with excitement. Gemma, surrounded by marines, feels their curious stares on her. One marine, sitting on her left, leans in to smell her hair. Gemma shifts uncomfortably, her body tense. The marine inches closer, drawn in by the scent. Gemma's discomfort grows, her body scrunching up as she tries to create distance.

With a raised eyebrow, she asks, "Haven't you guys ever seen a girl before?"

The marine responds with a sly smile, "Not one that smells like you, sugar."

Gemma can feel his presence invading her personal space and she tenses up even more. The tension in the air is intense as Gemma tries to assert herself, but the marine's actions only make her feel more uneasy.

As the U.S. Marine truck approached the Garden Island gates, Gemma, Mark, and Ben peered through the window.

They could see two Australian guards standing duty at the entrance. A sign read "Garden Island: Restricted," hinting at the strict security measures in place.

"Oh great," Duane muttered, his face contorting in disgust.

"What's wrong?" Mark asked.

"It's diarrhea," Duane replied, his tone dripping with disdain.

"Diarrhea?" Mark repeated, confused.

"Yeah, he goes through everybody," Duane explained, his frustration clear.

Not wanting to get caught, Duane quickly instructed the trio to duck under a nearby tarpaulin. They scrambled onto the floor and squeezed under the covering, trying to remain hidden. Just then, the truck came to a stop as it reached the guards at the entrance.

Guard Bennett stood at the front of the truck, barking orders at the group of marines inside. He motioned for them to exit the truck, his tone stern and commanding. Meanwhile, Guard Robinson jumped into the back of the truck, brandishing his bayonet. He aggressively poked at the tarpaulin covering the cargo, his eyes scanning for any signs of trouble. He spotted a mop of blonde hair beneath the tarp and immediately grew suspicious. Duane nervously approached the exit tray and peered inside. Guard Robinson stood over the suspicious lump; his weapon pointed at it menacingly.

"I'll give you one chance," Robinson growled, "give up now, or I'll knife you."

There was no response from under the tarp.

"This is your last chance," he warned, "I'll count to three."

Duane couldn't stand by and watch as Robinson prepared to harm someone. He spoke up, pleading with him not to take any drastic action. But Guard Robinson was determined. He began to count, his eyes scanning the faces of the marines gathered around. They all looked worried and concerned.

"One... Two..."

Suddenly, Robinson hesitated. He looked around at his fellow guards and the marines, unsure of what to do. Then, with a burst of energy, he repeatedly stabbed the tarpaulin with his bayonet. Duane cried out in horror as Guard Robinson finally lifted a section of the tarp. Instead of a person, they were met with a rag doll riddled with holes from the bayonet.

Guard Robinson was taken aback, unsure of what to make of the strange sight. "What the hell is this?" he exclaimed.

A voice from outside the truck answered, "A guy's got to have a hobby."

All eyes turned to a sleazy looking marine standing outside.

Guard Bennett shook his head in disgust. "You're one sick pup," he muttered.

The sleazy marine chuckled, "Thanks a lot, man. You just killed Betty Grable!"

Guard Bennett and Guard Robinson exchanged bemused glances and shook their heads. The sleazy marine picked up the remains of the rag doll and continued his strange hobby.

Bennett Guard tried to justify their actions. "You Yanks smuggle stuff in here all the time. We're just doing our job."

But Marine Stuart couldn't stay silent any longer. "You guys are over the top!" he exclaimed.

Guard Bennett yelled for everyone to get back on the truck and continue with the task at hand. The marines reluctantly climbed back on board, the incident leaving a sour taste in their mouths. As they rode away, Duane couldn't help but feel a sense of unease at the strange events that had just unfolded.

The truck grinds to a halt at the boat dock, its engine growling as it comes to a stop. With a swift leap, Duane lands in the back of the vehicle. He eagerly lifts the lid of a long wooden bench seat, revealing three figures huddled inside. Gemma, Mark and Ben are cramped in the small space, their faces contorted with discomfort.

"Are you guys okay in there?" Duane asks, concern laced in his voice.

Gemma scoffs, trying to keep her composure. "Oh, we're just living the high life," she replies sarcastically.

The marines help the trio out of their cramped quarters, their movements swift and efficient. Duane chuckles as he watches them, a knowing smile on his face.

"This isn't the first time we've had to use this hiding spot," he remarks, his voice tinged with amusement.

Gemma raises an eyebrow, an smirk playing on her lips. "So, you guys smuggle in girls, too?"

Duane's smile turns wry. "Smuggle? A Southern gentleman wouldn't resort to such tactics."

Gemma's eyes light up with realization. "Wait, so what was that just now?"

Duane's grin widens. "Just helping out with our cultural exchange program. You show me yours and I'll show you mine."

Gemma's face breaks into a mischievous grin.

"Seriously?" Duane nods, his eyes sparkling with excitement. "You show me how to skateboard and we'll show you our boat."

Gemma's grin turns into a wide smile. "Let's do it!"

Duane looks at Ben, who is shaking his head in frustration.

"What did she say?" he asks, his voice laced with confusion.

"We need subtitles for these guys," Ben mutters, shaking his head in disbelief.

*   *   *

It was a hot afternoon at the dock on Garden Island in 1942. Duane strutted assertively up the gangplank of the *U.S.S. Chicago*, with Mark and Ben following nervously behind in their crisp U.S. Marine uniforms. Gemma, disguised as a mechanic, wore an oversized jumpsuit and a false moustache, her hair tucked under a cap. She kept her head down, trying to blend in.

As they reached the top of the gangplank, they saluted the sentry standing guard. Gemma's nerves got the best of her, and she crashed into a pole, tumbling backwards onto the deck.

The sentry rushed to her aid, noticing her unfamiliar smell. "Are you alright?" he asked, "You smell kinda different."

Gemma, still trying to maintain her disguise, spoke in a deep voice. "I'm fine," she said, brushing off the incident. "Must be those fumes below."

She caught up with the others, relieved that her Calvin Klein perfume was doing its job.

"We should have messed you up and made you real man-stinky," Ben joked.

Gemma rolled her eyes. "You could be my role model for sure."

Duane took charge and directed the group to head down to the engine room and then up on deck. As they walked, they ducked and held onto their caps as they passed through a large iron cabin door. The setting was bustling with activity, with sailors and marines scurrying around the deck. The smell of the ocean and the sound of waves crashing against the ship filled the air.

"Watch your heads!" Duane warned as they made their way through the narrow corridors.

The clanking of pipes and the roar of the engine room echoed through the ship. Gemma couldn't help but feel a sense of awe and excitement as they explored the inner workings of the *U.S.S. Chicago*.

Duane, Mark, Ben, and Gemma stepped out of the door, onto the deck. The intense heat hit them like a punch in the face, causing them to sweat profusely. They gasped for air; their shirts drenched in sweat. Mark declared it was hotter than hell, to which Ben replied that hell wasn't that hot.

Gemma wondered how the sailors managed to work down there. As they made their way towards a gun turret, they came across Pete, a rigid and orderly sailor, meticulously cleaning a gun that was already spotless. Duane couldn't help but comment on Pete's dedication to his gun. Pete replied that it was a matter of pride, and his eyes landed on Gemma. He couldn't help but notice her unbuttoned boiler suit, revealing her sweaty cleavage and bikini top. Gemma quickly buttoned up, feeling uncomfortable under Pete's gaze.

Duane led the group away, but Pete couldn't resist picking up the radio phone by the turret. In a hushed voice, Pete spoke into the phone, saying there was an intruder on the deck. He also mentioned her sweat and "wonderful boobs." As Gemma walked away, Pete's eyes followed her, unable to tear his gaze away.

The afternoon sun casts a warm glow through the small windows of the Communications Room on the *U.S.S. Chicago*. The radio operator grips his hand-held radio, his knuckles turning white. He glances around the room, searching for any sign of movement. His eyes darted back to the radio; his brows furrowed in frustration.

"Are you sure you haven't been polishing your weapon for too long?" the radio operator asks, his voice laced with annoyance.

Pete's voice crackles through the radio. "Just send Security to the deck," he says, clearly peeved.

The radio operator lets out a heavy sigh and scans the room once more. He knows he needs to find Security.

On the *U.S.S. Chicago* deck, four figures stood in a huddle, their backs to the approaching security guards. Gemma's eyes widened as she saw them coming.

"Where's your I.D.?" one of the guards barked at her, grabbing her forcefully and turning her around. He ripped open her boiler suit, exposing her cleavage.

"What the hell!" Gemma exclaimed, trying to cover herself.

The guard leered at her, his eyes lingering on her chest. "Well, well, what have we got here?" he said, smirking.

His crewmate joined in, ogling Gemma and making crude comments. "A nice set of boobies," he said, causing Gemma to cringe.

Without hesitation, the first guard yanked Mark and Ben away, while the second one grabbed Gemma.

"Shouldn't we search her?" he asked his partner, a sleazy grin on his face.

"Just take them below, you idiot," the first guard snapped, shoving Gemma towards the door.

Duane stepped forward, trying to defend Gemma, but the second guard blocked him with his rifle.

"I just wanted to show these good people over the *Chicago*—" Duane began but was cut off by the guard.

"Look Lieutenant, there's been a crackdown since you marines last smuggled in girls. Intelligence will want a word with them," the guard said, pushing Duane back.

Frustrated, Duane yelled to the time-traveling trio, "Sorry guys! I'll talk to a lawyer friend. He'll get you out!"

The rest of the security guards herded the trio along, their rough hands guiding them towards their fate.

Gemma, Ben, and Mark, all dressed in matching blue Navy brig uniforms, sit inside a cell aboard the *U.S.S. Chicago*.

The setting is bleak, with only the sound of the sea and the clanking of the cell doors adding to the tension. Gemma is slumped on the bed while Ben and Mark lay on the floor. The atmosphere is heavy with despondency. Ben's gaze falls on the cell opposite, where a burly, bald man sits cross-legged on the floor. He speaks to the man, trying to strike up a conversation.

"This prison life is getting old, isn't it?" Ben asks, trying to break the tension.

The brig prisoner responds, his voice laced with bitterness, "Lovers' quarrel," he says, his tone dripping with resentment.

Ben's concern is clear as he asks, "Must be tough on you?"

The prisoner's response is filled with anger and longing, "He got what he deserved when he didn't come across. It's lonely at sea sometimes. He knew how to press my buttons." Ben's agitation grows as the prisoner continues to talk, "The slight tilt of his hat; the little bow just slightly undone; the ass-hugging bell bottoms."

Feeling overwhelmed, Ben turns to Mark, his fear and frustration evident. "Get me out of here!"

CHAPTER 9

EPOCH

The streets of Woolloomooloo in 1942 were a chaotic mess, the aftermath of war still lingering in the air. As Duane rode in the front of a U.S. Navy Jeep with his marine driver, Mike, the scene outside was a constant blur of austerity and chaos. They were passing through the gates of Garden Island, a place that had become a symbol of hope and safety amidst the turmoil.

Suddenly, Duane's attention was drawn to an alley where two brutish men, muggers Clark and Davidson, had cornered an innocent man, Butch Bentley. With a ferocity that was all too common in these desperate times, they relentlessly kicked and beat him.

Duane's instincts kicked in, and without a second thought, he demanded, "Go back, Mike. That guy is getting mugged!" His words were urgent, his voice filled with concern for the man being attacked.

In a swift and decisive move, the Jeep made a sharp U-turn and raced towards the mugging scene. The tires screeched against the laneway pavement as they came to a sudden halt.

Butch lay on the ground, his body battered and broken from the vicious assault.

The air was thick with tension as Duane and Mike stepped out of the Jeep, ready to intervene. The setting was a stark reminder of the harsh reality of war, and every detail around them served as a reminder of the danger that lurked in every corner.

Mike raced towards the car's bonnet, leaping onto it with a fierce determination. He then launched himself at Clark, tackling him to the ground with powerful force. The mugger struggled to break free and eventually managed to scamper away, followed closely by Davidson who disappeared around the corner. Meanwhile, Duane knelt next to Butch, a concerned expression on his face.

"Hey man, are you okay?" Duane asked, his voice filled with genuine worry.

Butch groaned, his head feeling groggy from the attack. "They jumped me as I came around the corner," he muttered, trying to shake off the dizziness.

"Don't move, just stay there," Duane advised, placing a comforting hand on Butch's shoulder.

Butch slowly got to his feet and shook his head, trying to clear his mind. "Nah, I'm fine," he declared, determined not to show any weakness.

Duane's eyes narrowed in concern as he took in Butch's bruised and battered appearance. "What's your name, soldier?" he asked, trying to distract Butch from the pain.

"Butch Bentley," he replied, wincing as he felt a sharp pain in his jaw.

"Hey, you don't happen to know a Mark and Gemma Bentley, do ya?" Duane inquired, hoping to find some connection to Butch.

Butch shook his head, his mind still reeling from the attack. "No, never heard of 'em," he replied, his voice filled with confusion.

Duane nodded, understanding that Butch was in no state to talk.

"Listen Lieutenant, thanks a lot. You saved me," Butch said, grateful for Duane and Mike's intervention.

"You're welcome," Duane replied, a hint of pride in his voice. "Do you need a lift to the hospital?" he offered, noticing Butch's injured jaw.

Butch considered it for a moment before shaking his head, "Nah, I've got a 'turn out' tonight. Don't want to waste time waiting in a hospital," he explained, determined not to let the mugging ruin his plans.

Duane nodded, understanding Butch's priorities.

"Well, you're welcome to join us at our party," Butch offered, gesturing to Mike who was already getting back into their car.

Duane couldn't help but smile at the offer, "Thanks mate, I really appreciate it," he replied, feeling grateful for the unexpected kindness from the Australian soldier.

As Duane and Mike drove off, Butch was approached by a young couple, Jess and Tim, who had witnessed the mugging from a distance.

* * *

The *U.S.S. Chicago* is bustling with activity on this sunny afternoon in 1942. In the brig, a young guard named Will sits at a desk, speaking on a hand-held radio. Next to him stands an older guard named Mel.

Will's eyes flicker with concern as he talks on the radio, trying to help his brother's struggling family back home. Mel signals him to end the call.

Without hesitation, Mel reaches over and turns off the radio, causing Will's anger to flare up.

"What the hell, Mel? That was my dead brother's widow. I'm just trying to make sure she's okay," Will exclaims.

"I don't care. I've told you before, there are no personal calls on the radio. Next time, I'm reporting you," Mel responds coldly before walking away.

Will shakes his head in disbelief.

Meanwhile, in the cell, Gemma lies on the bed as her eyes dart back and forth, listening intently to Will's conversation. Mark and Ben sit on the floor, while Duane approaches the bars. Will opens the cell door and Duane enters, bringing some unexpected good news.

"We're getting out?" Gemma asks hopefully.

Duane confirms the news, but with a catch—they must wait until tomorrow. Gemma grabs Duane's arm, grateful for his help.

"We owe you big time, Duane," she says. Duane brushes off their gratitude, mentioning that he recently stopped a mugging around the corner in Woolloomooloo. The name of the victim catches Gemma's attention—Bentley, same as hers.

"Butch, he said. What are the chances?" Duane adds with a chuckle.

As he walks away, Gemma's thoughts turn to her grandfather, who is scheduled to board the ship tomorrow. She turns to Mark and Ben, a grim, determined look on her face.

"We have to stop him from boarding that ship. Otherwise, he'll be killed," she says.

Realization dawns on them as they realize the consequences of their actions—if their grandfather dies, they will never exist.

Gemma's mind races as she comes up with a plan. A mischievous smirk spreads across her face.

***

The afternoon sun beat down on the *U.S.S. Chicago* as Will sat in a chair, engrossed in a comic book. Across from him, Mark, Ben, and Gemma were locked in a cell. Gemma stood at the bars; her eyes locked on Will.

"Excuse me, Will? It's Will, isn't it?" Gemma's voice broke through the silence.

Will looked up, his eyes meeting Gemma's. "Yep."

"Sorry to interrupt, but I couldn't help overhearing before. That's a fine thing you're doing for your sister-in-law," Gemma's words were filled with admiration.

Will leaned forward in his chair, a sense of pride swelling within him, "Thanks. What else am I supposed to do? My brother was killed in Guam. She's on her own with two small kids." He paused, then pulled out his wallet. "Want to see them?"

Gemma nodded eagerly; her curiosity piqued. Will stood up and proudly showed her a picture of his late brother's family.

"Cute kids," Gemma remarked. "You know, I would ignore that other guard. You keep calling her, they're important to you. You're doing the right thing by looking after them."

Will's eyes lingered on the photo, a look of love and determination in them. "How could I not?"

"I know," Gemma replied with a knowing smile. "We're in a similar situation with my sister's kids." Will's interest was piqued, and he moved closer to the cell. Gemma crossed her fingers behind her back, hoping her words would have the desired effect. "Our sister's husband was killed in action recently. They had kids," Gemma continued. "That's where we were headed to."

"You were?" Will's voice was filled with curiosity.

Gemma nodded; her eyes locked on Will's. "The kids are quite a handful. We were going with Mark, my brother, to help her with them. She's been sick, and it's really taken a toll on her. Poor thing."

Will's heart swelled with empathy for Gemma and her family. He paused, then glanced around before unlocking her cell, leaving the door slightly ajar.

"Wait for five minutes and then go. Remember, five minutes. No sooner," Will instructed.

Gemma's face lit up with gratitude. "Thank you. Look after your sister. You're a good guy."

As Will turned to walk away, he called out to Mel, a guard nearby. "Hey Mel, how about a game of cards? We'll play for who leaves early." With a sly smile, he opened a door beside the cells, leaving Gemma to make her escape.

Gemma's eyes fixate on the clock hanging on the wall of her cell. She glances over at Mark and Ben, her expression determined. Without hesitation, she motions for them to follow her lead. They nod in agreement and quickly make their way towards the cell door. With a swift push, they force it open and hastily gather their belongings from the lockers on the opposite wall. Gemma's heart races as she grabs her clothes, backpack, and duffle bag, each item representing a small glimmer of hope for their escape.

Will and Mel sat at the poker table in the Brig office, their faces displaying contrasting emotions. Will's eyes were fixed on the door, while Mel's gaze was directed at the wall.

Will's amusement grew as he saw Mark and Ben tiptoe by, waving cheekily. Mark struggled to carry the heavy duffle bag, but it didn't seem to bother him.

"What's got you smiling, Will?" Mel inquired, breaking the silence.

"Just thinking about how easy it is to bluff you," Will responded, a sly smile playing on his lips. He glanced down at his cards, a confident look on his face. The sound of the cards shuffling, and chips clinking filled the room, adding to the tense atmosphere. The dim light and the smell of cigars hung in the air, creating a strong sense of the ruse occurring on board the mighty *U.S.S. Chicago.*

Mark and Ben strolled down the gangplank, saluting the sentry at the top as they passed.

Suddenly, the sentry's voice broke through the air. "Hey, wait!" he called out.

The boys turned hesitantly, their bodies tense with nerves as the sentry hurried down the walkway towards them.

"You dropped this," he said, handing Mark a lipstick. Mark's face flushed with relief as he took the lipstick.

"Thanks," he said with a grateful smile. "My girl can't go a day without it."

The sentry's expression softened.

"Have a good time on leave, guys," he said before bounding back up the walkway.

Mark wiped his brow, feeling the tension in his body dissipate.

The familiar smell of the sea and the sound of the waves crashing against the dock filled his senses, reminding him of the calm before the storm. He looked over at Ben, who was taking in the sights and sounds of the bustling dockyard. But as they made their way towards the exit, Mark couldn't help but feel a sense of unease. The war was raging on, and they were just a small part of it.

A nearby alley was dark and musty, the only light coming from the dimming sun. Mark and Ben cautiously made their way into the alleyway, their eyes darting around for any sign of danger. Mark gently placed the duffle bag on the ground, carefully unzipping it to reveal its contents. Gemma, who had been coiled up inside, quickly hopped out.

"Your ass was constantly hitting my head," Gemma grumbled, rubbing her sore head.

Mark winced in pain, grabbing his backside. "Well, I have the bruises to prove it."

Ben looked around, his eyes searching for an escape route. "How do we get out of here?"

Gemma's eyes widened as she remembered their plan. "Duane."

* * *

The truck rumbled through the streets of Woolloomooloo, the sound of its engine drowning out any conversations. Duane sat on the bench-seat at the back, surrounded by his companions Mark, Ben, and Gemma. They were dressed in 1940s attire, blending in with the era they had traveled to.

Mark took a swig from his bottle of Budweiser, his face contorting with pleasure. The privacy flap was lowered, shielding them from the curious eyes of passersby. With every bump on the road, the group bounced along with the truck.

Duane's remorse was clear in his sincere tone as he spoke to his friends. "I'm really sorry you guys got locked up."

Gemma's response was dismissive, "Don't worry about it. We wanted to see the ship." She placed her hand on Duane's leg in a comforting gesture.

A smile crept onto Duane's face as he looked at Gemma, "Well, if there's any way I can make it up to you..."

Mark chimed in, "Getting us to Butch's place will do."

"Who is this Butch?" Duane asked, curious about the person who held such importance for his friends.

Gemma's reply was simple, yet poignant, "He's our grandfather. We can't exist without him."

Duane was taken aback by this revelation. "I don't understand how this can happen. But I believe you."

The anxious looks on Gemma and Mark's faces made Duane furrow his brow in confusion. The pieces of this puzzle were starting to come together, but there were still missing parts.

CHAPTER 10

STEALTH

The Tasman Sea was painted in shades of orange and purple as the sun began to set. The calm water stretched out before them, reflecting the beautiful sky above. A Japanese submarine, known as an A-class, floated steadily on the surface, its sleek metal body glistening in the fading light.

The captain of the submarine stood tall on the control tower deck; his gaze fixed on the horizon. Without a word, he reached for his radio, his actions speaking louder than any words could. He addressed his three midget submarines, *M27*, *M24*, and *M22*, that cruised ahead of him.

In a quiet and determined voice, he spoke to his lieutenant in Japanese, a language that carried the weight of his country's pride and honor. He reminded his crew that they were not alone in their mission, that the people of Japan and their Emperor stood behind them. With a salute, he showed his unwavering loyalty and respect.

The salty sea air filled the captain's lungs as he stood in silence, taking in the beauty of the moment. The gentle rocking of the waves beneath him and the distant sound of seagulls created a peaceful atmosphere. But beneath the tranquility, a sense of determination and purpose lingered, ready to be unleashed at any moment.

As the captain's words hung in the air, they were a reminder of the stakes at hand. The mission was not just about the physical act of war, but also about honoring one's country and those who stood behind them. And in that moment, the captain's actions and words spoke volumes, creating a strong sense of character.

As the sun slowly sets on the horizon, Lieutenant Chuma and Petty Officer Ohmori find themselves cramped in the tight confines of the *M27* midget submarine. They are lying on their stomachs, surrounded by the claustrophobic conditions of the vessel.

Lieutenant Chuma's eyes are fixed on the control panel in front of him. He reaches for the radio and speaks in a determined tone, his words in Japanese, "Thank you, Captain. Imperial forces will triumph, and the world will be a better place for our loved ones." He hangs up the radio and reaches for a photo of his wife and baby daughter, their smiling faces a source of comfort during their dangerous mission.

With a tender kiss, he places the photo next to the controls and whispers in Japanese, "Love you both. I'll be in your arms soon." His actions convey a deep sense of love and determination as he prepares for the mission ahead. Without hesitation, he throws two switches on the control panel and the engine roars to life, filling the small space with its powerful vibrations.

As the submarine begins to move, the only sounds are the throb of the engine and the muffled voices of Lieutenant Chuma and Petty Officer Ohmori. The tension and danger of their situation is profound, and their actions speak volumes about their bravery and loyalty.

The sun begins to set as Midget Submarine *M24* silently follows behind *M27* and *M22*, gliding effortlessly on the surface of the water. In the distance, the lights of Sydney Harbour can be seen.

The crew of *M24* hold their breath as they approach their destination. The sound of waves lapping against the hull and the faint hum of the submarine's engine are the only noises in the still evening air. As they draw closer to their target, the tension rises and the adrenaline pumps through their veins. The crew's eyes are fixed on their mission, their determination evident in their focused expressions. The scene is set for a daring and dangerous mission.

* * *

Back in Woolloomooloo, the marine truck pulled up to Butch's house, the rear flap opened, and Gemma, Mark, Ben, and Duane appeared. Mark wasted no time in opening a bottle of Budweiser and downing it.

Duane looked around and asked, "So, this is your Gramp's place?"

Mark glanced up at the build date on the facade and replied, "Yeah, it was built in 1886."

The group jumped out of the truck and surveyed the house. Gemma thanked Duane for getting them there, to which he jokingly responded, "For getting you guys locked up?"

She playfully brushed off his comment and continued, "No, silly. For bringing us here. You've been the perfect Southern gentleman. If only the timing had been different..." Gemma's gaze shifted to Mark and Ben, hinting at what could have been between them.

In a sudden burst of emotion, Gemma grabbed Duane's arms and passionately kissed him. Mark and Ben, feeling uncomfortable, looked away while the truck driver shook his head, muttering, "Those Texans always get the chicks."

Duane, still dazed from the kiss, grinned with delight and remarked, "They don't kiss like that back home."

As they made their way to the front door of No. 66, Mark suddenly stopped in his tracks.

"I'm having second thoughts," he admitted. "Is the old bastard really worth it? The guy is an asshole."

Gemma was appalled by his words and reminded him of the consequences if they didn't fulfill their mission. "He dies and we don't exist. We'd never be born," she pointed out. Reality dawned on Mark, and he looked grim as they approached the door.

Gemma knocked and the sound of an Andrew Sisters song playing on a gramophone could be heard inside. The door opened to reveal Alice, a kind, middle-aged lady. Party sounds and sights filled the room behind her.

"Can I help you?" she asked.

Gemma replied, "We're looking for Butch."

Alice was taken aback by the sudden appearance of the trio. Gemma and Mark threw their arms around her and hugged her tightly. She was confused and asked for their names.

The trio exchanged amazed looks and Mark whispered to Ben, "Our great-grandma!"

Gemma continued, "Ahh—Alice! It's so great to finally meet you. Kevin told us all about you!"

Alice seemed puzzled and said, "He's never mentioned you."

Just then, a tall and gangly soldier named Joe appeared behind Alice and ogled Gemma. "They're okay. Butch knows them," he said. Without hesitation, Joe grabbed Gemma's arm and pulled her inside. She followed cautiously as Mark and Ben entered behind her.

The lounge room was filled with a mix of soldiers and girls, all around the age of twenty. Their curious eyes followed as Joe, Gemma, Mark, and Ben entered. Gemma's modern 2007 hairstyle at once caught the attention of the women.

Mark surveyed the group of soldiers, trying to figure out which one was Pop.

"Which one is Pop?" Mark asked, looking around.

"I've never heard Butch called Pop before. It suits him though," Joe replied. "I'm Joe. What are your names?"

They all shook hands and introduced themselves. Gemma took the lead. "I'm Gemma, this is Mark and Ben. So where is Butch?"

Joe pointed in the direction of a handsome soldier with dark hair. Beside him was a man in a grass skirt playing a ukulele—Butch.

The trio approached the handsome soldier, their gaze fixed on him.

"Pop was a hottie when he was young," Gemma commented.

"His pictures never did him justice," Mark added.

"Did you expect anything less from a camera called a box brownie?" Ben chimed in.

But their admiration was short-lived when the handsome soldier spoke, "I'm not Butch, but he wishes. He's right next to you, playing the ukulele."

Disappointed, the trio turned their attention to Butch. He was sweating profusely as he strummed the ukulele on his table. His head was bruised from a recent mugging.

"Your Pop was a loser?" Ben blurted out, half-drunk.

Mark, with a beer can in hand, reached out and grabbed Butch's leg. "Hey Butch, nice party, man. We just wanted to say hi. Sorry about the mugging."

Butch jumped off the table and landed on Ben, causing them both to fall to the floor. Mark helped Butch up, while Ben slowly dusted himself off.

"G'day, I'm Butch," he said, introducing himself.

"Hey Butch, this is Gemma, that's Ben, and I'm Mark," Mark replied, still half-drunk.

"So—who did you blokes come with?" Butch asked, looking at them expectantly.

The trio hesitated, searching for an answer.

"Big Joe! He invited us," Gemma finally spoke up, blowing a kiss at Joe. Joe grinned and made an hourglass figure to Butch, while Gemma looked away.

"Big Joe's done alright for himself," Butch remarked.

"Yeah, he's—ahhh—big. Yep, he's big, our Joe," Gemma added, awkwardly.

"So where are you from?" Butch asked Mark.

"Bondi. We live in Bondi," Mark replied.

"I wouldn't mind living in Bondi," Butch said wistfully.

"You will," Mark replied confidently. Gemma hit Mark on the leg, causing him to yelp in pain.

"Is he alright?" Butch asked, concerned.

But Mark was too drunk to realize his faux pas. "So, where's Nellie?" he asked.

"Why do you want to know about Nell?" Butch's tone turned serious.

"She's your wife?" Mark asked, not understanding the situation.

"Nell's a nice girl, but I hardly know her. Mate, stay off the turps!" Butch walked off, perplexed and slightly annoyed.

"Nice one, Mark," Gemma scolded, annoyed. "You talked about things that haven't even happened yet. They don't get married for two more years!"

"Oh shit. I'm getting another beer," Mark muttered, embarrassed.

Gemma shook her head in disappointment, wishing Mark had more tact and awareness.

Mark stormed into the kitchen, his steps heavy and his face red with anger. He roughly opened the fridge and grabbed a beer from the ice in the sink. As he turned around, he was met with a young girl, Dot, who looked just like Rachel, the girl from the beach who had his shorts.

"Rachel?" Mark's voice was laced with confusion.

"I'm not Rachel. My name is Dot," the girl replied calmly, not showing any signs of recognition.

Mark's mind flashed back to the beach, to the girl jogging with her friend and picking up his boardies after they fell off.

"Did you time travel too?" he blurted out.

Dot's expression turned to one of perplexity, but also curiosity. "I have no idea what you're talking about. And I certainly don't know anything about time travel or your boardies," she replied, her tone slightly amused. "But," she added, "I've never heard that line before."

Mark suddenly realized his mistake, "Oh, my bad. I'm so sorry," he apologized, feeling embarrassed. "You just look exactly like someone I met on Bondi Beach before."

Dot smiled and shrugged it off. "No worries, I accept your apology. But what did you say about time travel?"

Mark hesitated, not wanting to reveal his strange thoughts. "Oh, it was nothing. I'm a writer and sometimes my imagination gets the best of me. You know, Jules Verne stuff."

The word "writer" caught Dot's attention. She looked thoughtful, seizing on it as an explanation for Mark's odd behavior.

"You're a writer? I love science fiction and fantasy," she said, laughing. "My friends think I'm weird for it. What do you write about?"

Mark tried to think of a fantasy subject to impress her. "Good versus evil, stories with hobbits, elves, and wizards in a place called Middle Earth."

Dot's interest was piqued. "What's your name?"

Mark hesitated for a moment before answering, "Tolkien." Coyly, he looked to the side.

"That's a Russian name, right?" Dot asked.

"Yeah, but my friends call me Mark," Mark replied with a small smile.

Dot extends her hand towards Mark with a friendly smile. "Hi Mark, I'm Dorothy, but you can call me Dot."

Mark glances around the room, trying to get a sense of his surroundings. "So, who are your friends with here?" he asks curiously.

"Just a friend of a friend," Dot responds nonchalantly. "The party host, Butch, is quite the character. His whole family is a bit odd."

Mark shrugs, "They're not bad once you get to know them."

Curiosity sparks in Dot's eyes. "So, Mr. Writer, have you had anything published?"

Mark hesitates, deep in thought. Suddenly, he has a revelation. "No, not yet. I'm working on a trilogy of books with the working title of Lord of the Rings."

"I'll keep an eye out for it," Dot responds with a smile.

"Tolkien, don't forget it," Mark adds, moving in closer to confide in her. "You know, Dot, you remind me of someone," Mark says, a hint of nostalgia in his voice.

Dot is touched by his words and takes his hand. "Oh, you mean your Rachel? Hopefully you'll get back to her soon."

Mark's expression darkens. "I don't know. I may never see her again."

But instead of feeling down, Dot's smile brightens, "I have a feeling that you will. I don't know why, but I'm sure you'll see her again."

Mark looks at her quizzically, but they both burst into laughter as Gemma interrupts them.

"I don't know why I said that," Dot says, still laughing. "But I mean it."

Gemma approaches Mark, pulling him away from Dot. "Can I have a word with you?" Apologizing to Dot, Gemma drags Mark towards the kitchen. "Look Mark, don't you remember why we're here? The Japs are torpedoing the *Kuttabul* tonight for Christ's sake!"

Mark scoffs, "So it's okay to flirt with a marine, but I can't even talk to someone?"

Gemma laughs, "Since when did you start kissing sailors?" They both share a laugh, their gazes falling on Butch as he makes silly noises into a sink full of ice and water. Two soldiers nearby joined in on the laughter.

"He needs all the help he can get," Mark comments with a smirk. Suddenly, Butch's head pops up, gasping for air and turning blue.

***

Meanwhile, the dark waters of Sydney Heads were eerily calm, disturbed only by the faint hum of three midget Japanese submarines passing through. Their periscopes silently glided atop the small swell, their presence a menacing threat.

In the cramped interior of the *M24* midget submarine, Lieutenant Ban peered anxiously through his periscope. In the distance, a buoy bobbed atop the water's surface. His sharp eyes could make out a net just fifty metres ahead.

"Surface! Surface!" he shouted urgently. His heart raced as he lowered the periscope, revealing a net stretching across the width of the Harbour, just three metres below the surface.

Underwater, the three Japanese submarines began to ascend. *M24* and *M22* successfully cleared the net, but *M27's* propeller caught in the mesh, causing it to spin uncontrollably.

Inside the *M27*, Lieutenant Chuma and Petty Officer Ohmori were drenched in sweat as they struggled to escape the net. Lieutenant Chuma strained to push the hand accelerator, but the submarine remained trapped.

"I'm giving it everything, but we're not moving. We're caught!" he yelled in frustration, reflecting the urgency of the situation.

"We can't reverse, there's no gears!" Petty Officer Ohmori exclaimed; his face twisted in anger.

Meanwhile, in the *M22*, Lieutenant Keiu Matsuo and Petty Officer Tsuzuku remained composed and focused as their submarine glided towards the surface.

"We've passed the net," Lieutenant Matsuo announced in Japanese, a sense of relief clear in his voice. As he peered through his periscope, he squinted at an impossibly bright floodlight that appeared in his vision, casting a harsh glare on the situation.

As a patrol boat lookout scans the dark waters of Sydney Harbour, a man named Roy with keen eyes, spots something moving below the surface. He raises his binoculars and aims them at the target, his heart racing with anticipation. With a swift motion, he points to the *M22* submarine lurking in the depths.

"Sir, midget sub on the bow, ten o'clock!" he calls out to the patrol captain.

Without hesitation, the patrol captain barks out orders. "Open up, Roy!"

Gunner Roy springs into action, his fixed machine gun blazing with fury. The shots light up the night sky as they rain down on the unsuspecting submarine.

Underwater, the *M22* is swiftly met with a barrage of bullets, piercing its hull with a deafening roar. Inside, Lieutenant Keiu Matsuo and Petty Officer Tsuzuku are jolted by the impact. The sound of rapid explosions fills the cramped space, causing the submarine to vibrate violently.

"Dive! Dive!" Lieutenant Matsuo shouts in Japanese, his voice barely audible over the chaos.

But before they can make a move, Petty Officer Tsuzuku is hit by shrapnel and falls to the floor, clutching his arm in pain. Lieutenant Matsuo's head drops in defeat, but then he slowly lifts it, determination etched on his face.

He reaches for a side compartment and pulls out a pistol, his fingers trembling with resolve. Turning to Petty Officer

Tsuzuku, he flicks a switch, plunging them into darkness and silence. In the stillness, the only sound is the faint clicking of the pistol's safety being released. Then, in a split second, two gunshots ring out, one after the other, shattering the quietness of the night. The impact of the shots reverberates through the submarine, a final act of defiance in the face of certain defeat.

CHAPTER 11

SECRETS

Back at Bentley Terrace, the moonlight spilled into the living room, casting shadows on the walls. Mark stumbled towards Butch, his breath reeking of alcohol as he clutched onto a bottle of beer.

"So, Butch. Are you on duty tonight?" Mark slurred, his words slurring together.

Butch's eyes narrowed; suspicion evident on his face. "Can't say for sure. You could be a spy for all I know." He took a swig from his own bottle, his grip tightening around it. "Loose lips sink ships, you know."

Mark chuckled, taking another swig. "So do midget subs."

Butch's eyebrows shot up in confusion. "What's that supposed to mean?"

Mark shrugged, his lips curling into a mischievous grin. "Nothing, just a saying."

Butch's gaze narrowed even further. "I don't know you from a bar of soap. But there's something about you that seems familiar."

Mark's expression turned frustrated, his brows furrowing. He couldn't shake off the feeling that Butch was onto him.

Ben sat on the worn, wooden steps of the neighboring house, a cold beer in his hand. Nell, a blonde girl with a sweet smile and a vintage haircut, joined him. She asked him about Butch, and he told her he was there with his friends, Mark and Gemma, who happened to be Butch's grandchildren. Nell looked puzzled, but Ben's playful expression made her laugh.

"You're funny," she said. "I like that about you."

"Who else do you like at this party?" Ben asked, a mischievous glint in his eyes.

Nell hesitated, blushing. She didn't know him well enough to share her secret.

"It's embarrassing," she said. "I sort of have a crush on Butch."

Ben's smile widened. "Really? Butch? The loud, kinda fat guy? What do you like about him?"

Nell's cheeks flushed even more. "He's just...sweet. He cares about his family and friends. That's important to me."

Ben realized he didn't even know her name yet. "I'm Ben," he said, extending his hand.

"Nell," she replied, shaking his hand. "Nice to meet you."

"You're Butch's future—" Ben started, but quickly stopped himself, standing up with agitation.

"Future what?" Nell asked, feeling confused and slightly disappointed.

Ben's face was red, and he seemed anxious. "I gotta go," he said abruptly. "Nice meeting you, Nell." And with that, he rushed off, leaving Nell feeling miffed and wondering about the future he had almost mentioned.

In the dimly lit lounge room of Bentley Terrace, Gemma found herself cornered by Joe. She desperately tried to maneuver past him, but his large frame blocked her escape. She subtly pushed him aside, her eyes darting around the room for a way out.

"Let's put some music on," Gemma suggested, trying to diffuse the tension.

Joe's response was enthusiastic, "Yes, I'd like to get to know you better."

But Gemma had no intention of getting to know Joe any better. She pushed him harder, causing him to stumble backwards and knock over a table, spilling food and drinks onto the floor. Butch quickly appeared at Gemma's side.

"Are you alright?" he asked, concern etched on his face.

Gemma brushed off the incident, "I'm fine, but Joe's ego might be a little bruised."

Butch chuckled, "Yeah, that's big Joe for you." As he looked at Gemma, Butch recognized something familiar about her. "It's your eyes," he said, "I can't place it, but I recognize you."

Before Butch could finish his sentence, Ben suddenly appeared.

"Gem, can I see you for a minute?" he asked, pulling her away.

As Gemma walked away with Ben, Butch found himself approached by Mark, holding a beer bottle.

"So Butch, what do you do with your spare time?" Mark inquired.

Butch listed off his various activities, including sailing and playing rugby, and his aspirations to become captain of the Clovelly Surf Club.

"Give it a couple years and you'll make captain," Mark predicted confidently.

Butch was intrigued by Mark's statement. "How in the world could you know that?"

Mark took a step closer, his beer-fueled confidence evident. "Well, if I was a betting man, I'd say you'll do it in 1946 and 1950."

Butch was skeptical. "Turn it up! No one can tell the future."

But Mark was insistent. "I'll give you a tip, Butch. The war will end in 1945, and we'll win. The Yanks will build a bloody great atomic bomb. They'll drop it on two Jap cities, and they'll surrender."

Butch couldn't believe what he was hearing. "Atomic bomb?! You're crazy mate!!"

Gemma, who had been listening in on the conversation, couldn't hold back any longer and grabbed Mark's arm, pulling him away.

Ben and Mark stood facing each other, the air charged with tension. Mark's eyes widened as Ben's voice boomed, reminding him of time travel rule number two. Mark's mind raced as he tried to come up with a clever response, but Ben's stern expression told him that he had already revealed too much information.

Gemma, noticing Mark's unease, stepped in to diffuse the situation. She explained that Mark was a writer, prone to blending reality with fiction. Butch, confused by the mention of an atomic bomb, demanded an explanation. Gemma quickly grabbed Mark's beer and pulled him aside, scolding him for scaring off Butch with his talk of the future.

Mark defended himself, saying he was just trying to be friendly and get on Butch's good side. Gemma shook him by the arm, urging him to be more careful. She reminded him to plan to keep Butch from boarding the doomed boat.

Gemma gushes, "Ben ran into someone outside that might be able to help us."

"Who?" asked Mark, his curiosity piqued.

"Grandma!" exclaimed Gemma, her excitement clear in her voice. The two of them walked out, their hearts racing with anticipation.

The house sat next to Bentley Terrace, looming in the darkness of the night. Gemma's eyes flicked towards Nell, silently conveying a warning. Mark followed her gaze, his own curiosity piqued.

Gemma's hand tightened around Mark's arm as they cautiously approached Nell, careful not to reveal any hints of the future.

Nell, a young girl with a cute appearance, sat on the doorstep. Gemma and Mark stood in front of her, introducing themselves as friends of Ben.

"He's a funny guy," Nell giggled, playing with her curls.

"Is he funny ha-ha or funny weird?" Mark asked, unable to hide his confusion.

Nell grinned, "Funny ha-ha, silly. He's a nice boy."

Gemma complimented Nell's hair, admiring its resemblance to the iconic Andrew Sisters. Nell returned the compliment, noting Gemma's unusual hair.

"Can I hug you?" Gemma blurted out, surprising both Nell and Mark.

Nell hesitated, but eventually gave in to Gemma's embrace. Mark, feeling left out, asked if he could join in as well.

"Uh, I suppose," Nell replied, unsure of what was happening.

Gemma explained that hugging was a Bondi tradition, a family thing. Nell seemed to understand, but her attention was quickly diverted when Gemma mentioned dancing.

"Do you like to dance?" Nell asked eagerly.

Gemma's eyes lit up, "I love Hip-Hop and R&B."

Nell looked confused. "I've heard of the jitterbug, but not Hop-Hip. Is R&B like The Pride of Erin?"

Gemma shook her head, laughing, "No silly, Ben has an iPod. We'll show you."

Without hesitation, Gemma took Nell's hand and led her inside the house, excited to introduce her to the world of music and dance.

Ben kneels beside a gramophone, his fingers tracing the dusty grooves of the record. He pauses, deep in thought, before carefully pulling out wires from the gramophone's rear. With a confident smile, he plugs one of the wires into his iPod and turns up the volume.

The room is suddenly filled with thumping dance music, causing some of the guests to cover their ears in surprise.

Gemma and Mark are on the dance floor, their movements energetic and fluid. Dot and Nell watch from the sidelines, unsure at first but soon warming up to the infectious beat. Nell starts tapping her hand on her leg, mimicking Gemma's dance moves before joining her on the floor. Dot follows suit, and soon the rest of the guests are staring in amazement at the impromptu dance party.

A party soldier nods his head in approval. "It's almost tribal, isn't it?"

Ben grins, "You got it dude!"

Butch, who has joined the dancers, is not as skilled and his movements are wild and uncoordinated. He slaps the floor with his hands and tries to do the robot and pop and lock moves, causing Nell to burst into laughter.

Joe jumps onto the dance floor, trying to get close to Gemma. Butch, annoyed, grabs Joe's arm and pulls him back.

"Give it a break, Joe!"

Joe protests, "The music's in full swing, Butch. We're here to party—let her have some fun."

Butch throws right hook at Joe, knocking him out cold. Gemma looks on in shock as the other guests gather around Joe.

Surprisingly, Butch turns to Gemma with a satisfied smile. "I said, stay away from her, you're not going to have fun with her."

Gemma is touched by Butch's defense. "Butch, you defended me! Thank you!!"

Butch, however, is not in a celebratory mood. "He's been heading for that all night. I've had enough. I'm goin' back to the *Kuttabul*." He storms out of the front door, leaving the party in disarray.

Mark checks the clock on the wall. "Oh, great! He's going back to the boat, and it will be torpedoed in three hours. Got any ideas?"

Gemma's eyes light up with determination. "As a matter of fact, yes. Ben!" She calls out to Ben, and the trio huddles together, whispering their plan.

* * *

The night air was thick with the sound of distant laughter and the scent of cigarettes. Butch leaned against a tree, his cigarette burning bright in the darkness. Nearby, Gemma paced in front of Bentley Terrace, her fingers fiddling with the buttons of her blouse. She glanced over at Butch, her eyes dark and determined.

She approached him, her movements oozing with confidence and seduction.

"Butch," she purred, "I just wanted to thank you for standing up for me."

Butch shrugged, the corners of his mouth turning up in a small smile. "It was nothing."

Gemma's lips curved into a sly grin. "You know, you're quite the ukulele player."

Butch raised an eyebrow, a hint of skepticism in his voice, "Am I? I just play for fun."

Gemma's eyes widened with admiration. "You play like Jimmy Hendrix!"

Butch's expression turned to confusion. "Who?"

Gemma quickly explained, her words painting a picture of an extraordinary entertainer playing his ukulele with wild and unexpected techniques. "Playing with his teeth, behind his back, setting the ukulele on fire. That sort of thing."

Butch's brow furrowed, still unsure.

"I was wondering," Gemma continued, "if you could give me some lessons."

Butch's face fell. "I'd love to, but I have to board my boat by eleven."

Gemma's eyes narrowed as she tried to think of another way to spend time with Butch. "That's a shame," she said, her voice dripping with seduction, "I was hoping we could spend some time together."

She reached out to caress Butch's arm and hair, but he gently pulled away. "Gemma, I appreciate the offer, but my heart belongs to someone else."

Gemma's eyes widened in surprise. "Nell?"

Butch nodded, a soft smile on his face. "She's the most beautiful girl in the world. I'm still working up the courage to talk to her. You're a nice girl, but more like a sister to me. Is that weird?"

Gemma's heart swelled with emotion at her grandfather's loyalty and love for Nell.

Butch then excused himself, leaving Gemma alone with her thoughts. Mark and Ben appeared from behind the wall, their faces expectant.

"So, is he going to go with you?" Mark asked.

Gemma smiled and shook her head. "No, he loves Grandma."

Ben grinned mischievously. "Plan B, then?"

Gemma and Mark exchanged hesitant glances, then nodded in agreement.

CHAPTER 12

THE OCEAN'S GRASP

Back on the Harbour, The *M27* midget sub lay trapped in the depths of Sydney Heads. Its motionless rudder was now home to a group of small fish, calmly swimming through the murky waters. Ten metres below the surface, it was ensnared in the nets at the Harbour entrance, a prisoner of war in the ocean's grasp.

Inside the sub, Lieutenant Chuma's body was drenched in sweat, his face pressed against the control panel. He struggled to lift his head; his weakness evident. His eyes focused on the gauge, which glowed in a dangerous shade of red, signaling a critical situation.

Without looking at Lieutenant Chuma, Petty Officer Ohmori let out a breathless gasp. His body was heavy with exhaustion.

"We're almost out of oxygen," Lieutenant Chuma said in a calm but urgent tone.

The weight of their situation hung heavily in the air as Lieutenant Chuma and Petty Officer Ohmori exchanged a knowing glance.

"I can't go on," Petty Officer Ohmori breathed out, his words barely audible. "End it now—*aargh!*"

Lieutenant Chuma's eyes flickered to the depth charge button, his hand hovering over it. He turned to look at Petty Officer Ohmori, seeking his confirmation. In response, Petty Officer Ohmori placed a tired hand on Lieutenant Chuma's leg, a silent gesture of support.

Lieutenant Chuma's gaze drifted to the photo of his wife and child, a reminder of what he was fighting for. He hesitated for a moment, then with a heavy heart, he pressed the button. The deafening sound of the explosion filled the submarine as they both closed their eyes, their mission coming to an end. The Harbour erupted in a flurry of white bubbles as the depth charge sank outside the *M27*.

The midget submarine was no match for the powerful detonation, its fragile body torn apart in a violent display. The explosion echoed through the depths, while the surface above remained eerily quiet.

* * *

Back at Woolloomooloo, and Nell sat on the steps of Bentley Terrace, her heart racing as she waited in the darkness. Mark and Ben appeared from the door, their hurried steps echoing on the pavement. As they rushed past her, Ben's backpack was unzipped, causing his sweater to tumble to the ground.

Without noticing, Mark's mobile phone also slipped from his pocket, landing next to a nearby bush.

Butch sauntered out of the door a few moments later, carrying a duffle bag. Nell stood up, her body tense with anticipation. She made a small gesture, as if to say goodbye, but then hesitated, her mind racing with second thoughts.

Butch caught sight of Nell and flashed her a smile. He seemed about to say something, but then changed his mind and continued on his way.

In nearby Woolloomooloo Park, Mark crouched behind a tree, his heart racing as he waited for Butch to approach. He gripped the cricket bat tightly, ready for action.

As Butch drew near, Mark heard a rustle above him. He looked up to see Ben perched on a large branch, high in the tree. Ben's eyes met Mark's and he gave a slight nod.

Mark's palms were sweating as he waited for the perfect moment. He whispered to himself, "I can do this."

Butch walked past the tree and Mark raised the bat, but then he froze. Doubt and fear crept in, making him question his ability to go through with their plan.

"What are you doing? Hit him!" Ben's voice echoed in Mark's mind, urging him to act.

Butch noticed the voices and looked up into the tree, trying to find the source. Suddenly, an owl hooted and Ben's branch broke, causing him to tumble down. Butch was struck by the falling branch and fell to the ground, unconscious.

Ben and Mark hurried down from the tree and rushed to Butch's side. They looked at each other with a mix of relief and guilt. As they tended to Butch's injuries, Gemma arrived.

Dot also appeared, holding Ben's jumper, and saw the tied-up Butch. She was shocked and confused.

"It's not what it looks like, Dot," Gemma explained, but she knew she had to come clean. "Listen, this is going to sound crazy, but..." Gemma's voice trailed off as she turned to face Dot, bracing herself for what she was about to reveal.

* * *

Below Sydney Harbour, Lieutenant Ban's eyes flicked to the periscope, the only way for him to see the outside world from the cramped confines of the *M24* midget submarine. He quickly scanned the horizon, searching for his target in the darkness of the 1942 night.

As he peered through the lens, he heard a voice, speaking in Japanese. Ban's lips curled in frustration as he realized it was coming from the Australian patrol boat that had crossed his line of sight, blocking his view of the *U.S.S. Chicago*.

The warship was a formidable sight, its sheer size and intimidating weaponry commanding the attention of all who laid eyes on it. The deck was lined with imposing guns and cannons, a display of its power and strength.

"Move, you Aussie bastard!" Ban exclaimed, his frustration boiling over as he turned away from the periscope. He knew the success of their mission depended on getting a clear view of the *U.S.S. Chicago*, and the Australian patrol boat was standing in their way. As he moved back and forth in the cramped submarine, Ban's mind raced with the possibilities.

He had to find a way to get a clear view of the warship, or their entire operation would be a failure.

***

In chilly Woolloomooloo Park, Butch's body was tightly wrapped in bandages and ropes, his mouth silenced with tape. As he regained consciousness, his body squirmed with panic, but he soon realized that his struggles were pointless.

Gemma was in a heated discussion with Dot, who looked shocked and disbelieving. She urgently conveyed, "We have to stop Butch from boarding the *Kuttabul,* or he will die, along with twenty-one others and we will cease to exist."

Dot's face furrowed with confusion and doubt. "It's—it's just too unbelievable," she muttered.

Gemma persisted, "But we showed you our phones and the iPod. Doesn't that prove we come from the future?"

Ben handed Dot his phone, and she watched a video of a pop song by Britney Spears. "It's just so far-fetched. Do all singers look like prostitutes in your time?" Dot asked, still skeptical.

The trio nodded in agreement, a glimmer of understanding in Dot's eyes, "I have to admit, such technology is unimaginable at this time. And yet..." she trailed off, deep in thought.

Mark added, "It's been exactly sixty-five years since that night."

Gemma turned to Dot with a knowing look. "You used to work in a photo development lab, right? You understand the power of images better than anyone."

Dot nodded slowly. "Yes, but... "

Gemma held up her iPod, "There are hundreds of songs stored in here."

Dot's disbelief was slowly melting away. "Well, do you promise to release him first thing tomorrow?"

Gemma raised her hand to swear, and Dot took it, still unsure.

Mark suggested, "In the meantime, Dot should stay with us until tomorrow. For her safety and everyone else's."

Dot agreed, and a small smile appeared on her face as she and Mark exchanged a knowing look. "That's terrible about the *Kuttabul*. Twenty-one people lost their lives?" Dot exclaimed; her voice filled with sadness.

Ben's eyes hardened with determination. "It's a bloody tragedy. We must stop it!"

Gemma added, "It's our only chance to save Pop. But how can we possibly stop a midget sub? No one will believe us. We'll probably end up in jail. Again."

Mark joked, "Love that prison food."

Dot playfully swatted him on the arm.

CHAPTER 13

MUMMY

The Botanical Gardens stood tall, its lush greenery illuminated by the dim moonlight. Gemma, Mark, Ben, and Dot strolled through the gardens, their feet crunching on the fallen leaves. As they reached a hilltop, they stopped in awe at the breathtaking view of the Harbour. The city lights twinkled in the distance, and the sound of waves crashing against the Harbour shore filled the air.

Gemma turned to her companions, a sly smile on her face, "We can sleep here, right?"

Dot glanced around, taking in the peaceful surroundings. She plopped down on the grass and gazed up at Gemma. "What about Butch?"

Gemma chuckled, gesturing to the snoring bandaged soldier under a nearby tree, "He'll be fine."

Ben suddenly announced, "I need to go piss."

Mark teased, "Be careful of the ferocious ducks."

A lone duck waddled towards Ben, causing him to retreat to a nearby tree. As he did, he passed by a sign with a pointer that read: "GARDEN ISLAND NAVAL BASE." The night was filled with the sounds of nature and the soft chatter of the group. The smell of fresh grass and salty sea air lingered in the air. As they settled down for the night, the city lights continued to twinkle in the distance, casting a warm glow over the botanical gardens.

With the group distracted, Butch's eyes fluttered open, his body jolting as he struggled to break free. Determination etched onto his face, he rolled away from the tree and down the hill. His eyes lit up with excitement as he made progress, giggling in delight.

Meanwhile, Mark lay awake on the grass, his eyes darting as he listened intently. Dot sat nearby, watching him closely.

With each bump and turn, Butch gained momentum as he rolled over the grass, hitting wood and splashing through rainwater. His moans and grunts mixed with the sounds of nature, creating a symphony of chaos.

Unable to control his movements, Butch tumbled uncontrollably to the bottom of the hill and onto the wharf. Muffled yells escaped from beneath the tape covering his mouth.

"Stop!" Butch cried out; his voice barely audible. As he teetered on the edge of the wharf, Butch slowly came to a halt. Breathing a sigh of relief, he gazed out at the dark waters of the Harbour, now covered in mud from his wild roll.

He heaves a sigh of relief as he stares at the darkness of the Harbour, filthy from his muddy roll. Most of the bindings have broken around his legs and loosened around his arms. Butch maneuvers himself onto his feet, and backs onto a wharf pole. He gazes at Garden Island and stumbles along the path with a halting, lop-sided walk.

Nearby, Sailor Len and girlfriend Jan lay on the soft grass, surrounded by twinkling stars. They embraced in a tender kiss, their bodies entwined as they gazed up at the night sky.

"Oh, Len, I wish we could stay like this forever," Jan said with a dreamy sigh.

Len chuckled; his arm wrapped around her, "Yeah, it's been a great night. That *Curse of the Mummy* movie was pretty scary, huh?"

Jan rolled her eyes playfully. "You only took me so you could hold me and make out."

"Well, it worked, didn't it?" Len grinned.

Their intimate moment was interrupted by a strange grunting noise coming from the nearby bushes. Len's body tensed as he looked towards the source of the sound.

"What the hell was that?" he asked, his voice filled with alarm.

Jan's eyes widened with fear. "You better go check."

Suddenly, a figure appeared from the shadows, shuffling towards them with muffled grunts. Len and Jan screamed as they saw Butch, still wrapped in tape and resembling the Mummy from the movie they had just seen.

"It's the Mummy!" Len exclaimed, his heart pounding in his chest. "He's come after us!"

"We can't kill him. It's thousands of years old," Jan added, her voice trembling with fear.

Len sniffed the air, his senses on high alert, "And he smells like it too."

As Butch stumbled towards them, Len pulled Jan closer, protectively wrapping his arm around her.

"He wants our life-source," Len explained, his voice filled with dread, "He's going to suck us dry."

Jan recoiled in disgust, "Ew, seriously Len?"

"He's going to kill us! Right, Jan. On the count of three, we run," Len said, his voice determined. "One...two..."

Without hesitation, Jan and Len jumped to their feet and ran as fast as they could until they were out of sight.

Butch stopped in his tracks, sighing sadly as he watched them go.

* * *

Butch stumbles along the Woolloomooloo Wharves, his steps unsteady and his movements clumsy. The loading docks stretch out before him, empty and silent. The gates of Garden Island Naval Base loom ahead, guarded by a solitary post. In the distance, *H.M.A.S. Kuttabul* rises from the dark waters of the Harbour.

Without warning, Butch's foot catches on an unseen obstacle and he tumbles to the ground. The wooden steps give way beneath him, and he plunges into the icy water below.

The guard post on Garden Island Naval Base is shrouded in darkness as night falls. Neville, the sentry on duty, is indulging in a hearty meal of pie and peas. Suddenly, a loud splash interrupts his contented munching, and he freezes, listening intently. After a moment of uncertainty, Neville shrugs nonchalantly and resumes his meal with gusto.

Butch plummeted towards the wharf supports, his body twisting and turning in a desperate attempt to slow his descent. He landed on his back with a thud, his eyes closing in resignation. A muffled splash echoed from above as he lay there, waiting for the inevitable. Suddenly, his eyes snapped open as he felt himself being pulled upwards. Confused, he looked to his side and saw the water swirling around him, carrying him towards the surface.

With a snort, Butch broke through the water's surface and desperately gasped for air. He could hear Mark's splashes behind him as his friend caught up. Together, they both gulped in precious oxygen, their bodies saturated and breaths coming in ragged gasps.

Mark's exhaustion was clear as he awkwardly pushed Butch onto the lower wharf landing. Pulling himself out of the water, he knelt above his young grandfather, their breaths still heavy and labored. The setting was peaceful yet tense, the sound of lapping water and heavy breathing filling the air.

Mark's eyes widen with excitement as he looks out to the ocean. He takes a deep breath and says, "It's not time for Neptune's playground yet, Mr. Roly Poly." He turns to Butch, a mischievous grin on his face. "You always did love the water, Butch." Mark hesitates, his mind racing with thoughts. "You know, in a few years, you'll be a lifeguard, patrolling Clovelly Beach. You'll save lives, like that father and daughter who will be drowning in the breakwater." Mark pauses, his voice serious now. "Just another reason to save you, Pop. You've got a lot more living to do and people to save. Maybe me, too."

Butch looks confused, trying to make sense of Mark's words. Mark lifts Butch onto his shoulder, his body tense with determination.

"I know you too, kid," Butch says, his voice dazed and distant.

Suddenly, a voice interrupts their moment.

"Hold it! Turn slowly," the sentry's voice rings out, breaking the tense atmosphere.

Mark stops and turns, setting Butch down gently. He raises his hands in the air, Butch's mouth now free from tape. The sentry aims his rifle at Mark's head.

Butch speaks up, trying to explain the situation. "I'm not a mummy! Nev, it's me, Butch. Butch Bentley!"

The sentry's face softens as he recognizes Butch. "Butch! Why are you wrapped up like a wounded corpse?" the sentry asks, lowering his gun.

Butch quickly rips off his bandages, revealing his face. The sentry's eyes widened in surprise.

"This loony tune tied me up," Butch explains, pointing to Mark. "He's some kind of 'clairvoyant.' Thinks he can see the future."

The sentry nods understandingly. "I had an auntie like that," he says.

Butch interrupts, urgency in his voice, "Bugger your Auntie. Give me a hand!"

The sentry reaches out and helps Butch to his feet, keeping his rifle pointed at Mark.

Mark speaks up, his voice wild and erratic. "I promise to go back to the nice padded white place and take some happy-happy pills."

The sentry looks from Mark to Butch, a look of sympathy in his eyes.

"Promise? You'll go straight back?" the sentry asks.

"Cross my liver and hope to die," Mark says, crossing his heart and raising his hand. The sentry smiles, feeling sorry for Mark.

"Alright, off you go then, young sparrow," the sentry says, gesturing for Mark to leave.

Mark starts skipping off into the night, singing, "They're coming to take me away ho, ho! They're coming to take me away ho, ho."

Butch and the sentry watch him go, perplexed.

"He was rambling about 'anemic' bombs and the war ending in 1945," Butch says, shaking his head.

The sentry shrugs. "The way the Japs are going in New Guinea, I doubt it. Anemic bombs? You mean *atomic* bombs?" he asks, his tone skeptical. Together, they turn and walk towards the entrance of Garden Island.

Mark crouches down behind a car, concealed from view by the Garden Island perimeter fence. In the distance, two soldiers and their girlfriend's approach, laughing and singing, each with a beer in hand. Soldier Portlock glances around to make sure no one is watching before lifting a section of wire at ground level. Mark watches intently from his hiding spot.

Soldier Portlock speaks with a sly grin, "This little trick buys us a few more hours of drinking." He chuckles and gestures for his girlfriend to go first. She drops to the ground and crawls, her backside sticking up in the air as she slips under the wire.

Soldier Portlock admires her shapely figure as she crawls, while Soldier Messing grins in agreement.

Nancy, Messing's girlfriend, playfully slaps him. "You better not try that with me," she teases.

Soldier Messing responds confidently, "I'll do more than that, darlin'." He grabs her behind, causing her to wiggle away and giggle.

Mark watches the scene unfold with a knowing smile.

The Botanical Gardens lay still in the darkness of the night, a peaceful haven amidst the chaos of war. Gemma's body tossed restlessly on the unforgiving ground; her mind unable to find respite from the trials of the day. Next to her, Dot snuggled close to a towering tree, finding solace in the comforting presence of nature. The night was alive with the sounds of nature, a symphony of rustling leaves, chirping crickets, and distant howls. And in the midst of it all, two weary souls found a moment of respite, a moment of quiet amidst the chaos, a moment of solace in each other's presence.

In the depths of the night, aboard *H.M.A.S. Kuttabul*, a row of Australian and British soldiers and sailors lay in their bunks, peacefully slumbering. Butch, dressed in army pants and a jumper, yawned and stretched before climbing into his bunk. As he settled in, his gaze turned towards the ceiling, and he closed his eyes. The stillness below deck was only broken by the sound of his soft breathing. The cramped quarters of the bunk room were a stark contrast to the vast expanse of the Harbour surrounding them.

The moonlit waters of Sydney Harbour glistened, casting an ethereal glow over the stillness of Garden Island. A small dingy silently cut through the water, its oars expertly maneuvered by Ben. As he approached the *U.S.S. Chicago*, his eyes scanned the looming destroyer, its imposing presence sending shivers down his spine. He knew he had to act, to save Butch on board the *H.M.A.S. Kuttabul*. Ben could feel the weight of the situation, the urgency of his mission.

"I won't let him die," Ben said, his voice resolute as he gazed up at the monolith-like destroyer.

CHAPTER 14

ATTACK!

The *M24* midget submarine glided silently through the dark waters of Sydney Harbour, its crew of two on high alert.

Lieutenant Ban stood at the periscope, scanning the area for any signs of their target. His eyes narrowed as he spotted a small rowboat in the distance, dwarfed by the imposing *U.S.S. Chicago* looming over it.

"Sir, the patrol boat is gone," Lieutenant Ban muttered in Japanese, his gaze fixed on the rowboat. "But what's this? Just some weird little guy in a tiny dinghy?" He turned to his companion, Namori, and gave the order, "Torpedoes ready!"

Namori quickly punched a button, his movements precise and efficient. As the *M24* midget submarine continued its stealthy approach, Lieutenant Ban's attention was drawn to his radar display. The *U.S.S. Chicago's* signal suddenly shifted to a different position.

"What the hell?" Lieutenant Ban exclaimed; his confusion evident in his voice. "The *Chicago* has moved. Move five degrees to starboard!"

Without hesitation, Namori adjusted the wheel, following his commander's orders. Meanwhile, on the rowboat, Ben had stopped rowing and pulled out his mobile phone. His fingers hovered over the keypad as he stared at the screen, which displayed the name "Gemma" and a series of numbers.

But suddenly, the phone beeped, showing no signal. Ben let out a frustrated sigh and hit himself on the side of the head.

"What am I doing?" he muttered to himself. "It doesn't work. I'm a dope."

The *M24* midget submarine prowled through the dark waters of Sydney Harbour, its radar and periscope searching for a target. Lieutenant Ban's eyes flicked between the instruments and the water outside, anticipation building in his gut. He whispered to himself in Japanese, a smirk playing on his lips as he spotted his prey.

"Come to momma, baby," he murmured, his fingers itching to press the firing button. With a swift motion, he pounded the button and a small torpedo shot out from the side of the submarine, surrounded by a cloud of bubbles. It glided smoothly under the water's surface, heading towards its target with deadly precision.

Meanwhile, on Garden Island, Ben rowed through the quiet night, his senses on high alert for any sign of danger. His heart raced as he spotted the torpedo, just fifty meters away on the water's surface. Panic seized him as he realized it was on a direct collision course with his dinghy.

"Shiiit!" Ben cursed, frantically rowing in a futile attempt to escape. But the torpedo was too fast, too close. In a split-second decision, he abandoned the oars and leapt into the water. He watched in terror as the torpedo grazed his dinghy and continued its path towards the *U.S.S. Chicago.*

With bated breath, Ben treaded water, his eyes fixed on the approaching vessel.

"Please, please don't hit the patrol boat," he pleaded, his heart pounding in his chest.

But just when it seemed certain that the torpedo would strike, it veered off at the last moment, skimming dangerously close to the ship's side before coming to a stop on the rocks.

Ben let out a shaky breath, relief flooding through him as he watched the failed torpedo.

The sound of blaring sirens fills the air as searchlights arc across the dark sky. A Patrol Boat Lookout peers through his binoculars, his eyes widening as he spots a torpedo on the rock. Immediately, he sets off the alarm, the loud bellows echoing through the night. Without hesitation, he reaches for his radio to alert the rest of the crew.

"Break! Break!! We got a sub in here. He's torpedoing the *Chicago!*" the Patrol Boat Lookout urgently reports into the radio. "Gunner to the deck, now! The Japs are attacking us!"

A door swings open and the Gunner appears, his eyes determined as he rushes to the turret. Swiftly, he cocks the mounted machine gun, ready for action.

"Where's the little shit?" he demands.

"Over there, to starboard," the Patrol Boat Lookout points.

Without a second thought, the Gunner swings in the direction indicated and fires round after round. The sound of gunfire fills the air as the two men work together to defend their ship.

As the chaos continues, Ben scrambles onto his dinghy, his heart racing as he tries to escape the danger. The scene is filled with the sounds of sirens, searchlights, and gunfire as the intense battle rages on.

The night was filled with chaos and danger as sirens blared and gunfire echoed through the air. Nell and Alice quickly sought refuge under a table in the dark kitchen of Bentley Terrace. Nell's hands instinctively covered her ears as Alice held her tightly, their hearts racing in fear.

Alice's worried expression spoke volumes as she whispered, "We have to pray for Kevin's safety."

Nell's mind was racing with concern, especially for Kevin (Butch) who was on the boat amidst all the chaos.

In a moment of desperation, Alice clasped her hands together in prayer and crossed herself, the only source of hope in such a dire situation. Nell held onto her tightly, finding solace in their shared fear and faith.

Amidst the deafening sounds of destruction, the two women found comfort in each other's embrace, their actions speaking louder than any words could convey. But in that moment, all that mattered was their bond and their strength to face whatever came their way.

***

The *M24* midget submarine glides silently through the dark waters of Sydney Harbour in 1942. Lieutenant Ban peers through the periscope, his eyes scanning the surface for any sign of danger. Suddenly, shots ring out and bullets splash into the water, narrowly missing the sub. Lieutenant Ban turns to Namori, their faces reflecting the tension and fear of the moment.

"They're firing at us!" Lieutenant Ban says in a hushed voice, "Five degrees to port, this time."

Namori expertly steers the sub to the left, narrowly avoiding the next barrage of shots. Lieutenant Ban looks through the periscope again, his expression determined and focused.

"We're ready," he says, "And firing two."

With a swift movement, Lieutenant Ban hits the launch button, and a torpedo is fired from the *M24*, disappearing into the murky depths of the Harbour.

As the torpedo powers away under the surface, the Patrol Boat Lookout watches its path through his binoculars. His face twists into a look of horror as he realizes its trajectory.

"Oh, dear God!" he exclaims, turning to the Patrol Boat Captain. "It's going to miss the *Chicago.* but it's heading for the *Kuttabul!*"

The Patrol Boat Captain's face pales as he grabs his radio and urgently calls out to the *Kuttabul.*

"*Kuttabul,* do you read me?" he shouts into the radio. "This is P.B.7. Incoming torpedoes! Incoming torpedoes!" The tension and urgency in his voice is intense as he waits for a response, the fate of the *Kuttabul* and its crew hanging in the balance.

The *Kuttabul's* bridge door creaked open, revealing the disheveled captain. His tired eyes were barely visible under the brim of his trench coat. He let out a long yawn as he made his way to the radio, his movements sluggish and heavy.

"*Kuttabul,*" he grumbled into the radio, "Is this a drill?"

But his question was interrupted by the urgent voice of the Patrol Boat Captain. "Abandon ship! Torpedo incoming on your bow!" The captain's voice crackled through the radio, "This is no drill. This is not a drill! INCOMING!!!!"

The *Kuttabul* captain's eyes widened as he processed the information. He quickly put on his glasses and squinted, his heart racing as he spotted the torpedo in the water ahead.

"SHIT!" he exclaimed, panic rising in his voice, "Abandon ship! Abandon ship! God help us!"

The sounds of sirens filled the air as the captain ran to the door, the chaos of the Harbour now reaching his ears.

Outside, the dark night was lit up by the explosion as the torpedo slammed into the *Kuttabul's* port side. The boat ripped open, sending a cloud of bubbles into the air as it sank beneath the water's surface.

The sound of a torpedo explosion reverberates through the Bentley Terrace kitchen, causing cups and saucers to shatter and a cabinet to crash to the ground. Nell's grip tightens around Alice's waist, her distress clear in her trembling body.

"We should have moved out west when the war began," Nell says, her voice filled with regret.

Alice shakes her head, her eyes filled with determination. "I'd rather meet my end here than move to Parramatta," she declares.

Nell's face contorts in disbelief at Alice's words. "So, you'd rather be buried six feet under than live out west?!" she exclaims.

Alice takes Nell's hand in hers, her touch gentle yet firm. "This is our home, Nellie. I'd rather leave in a pine box than be forced to move from my home," she says, her voice unwavering.

Another explosion rocks the ground, causing Nell and Alice to flinch and hold onto each other tightly. The distinct smell of smoke fills the air, and the kitchen is filled with the sound of chaos. But amidst it all, Nell and Alice stand strong, their love for each other and their home giving them the strength to weather the storm.

The Harbour was a battleground, the surface calm but the depths turbulent. A burst of flames erupted from below, ripping through the waterline of the *Kuttabul*.

Inside the cramped *M24* midget submarine, Lieutenant Ban and Namori stood shoulder to shoulder, their eyes fixed on the periscope. Without a word, Ban gestured towards the enemy ship. Namori's hand tightened on Ban's shoulder, his excitement unmistakable. The two exchanged a look of determination, their actions speaking louder than words.

With a triumphant yell, Namori pumped his fist in the air, "BANZAI!!"

The intensity of the moment was felt in every movement, every breath, and every exchange between the two men. This was a pivotal moment in the war, and the impact of their actions was experienced in every inch of the submarine.

***

Below the *Kuttabul* deck, the air is thick with chaos and the constant rumble of explosions. As the ship shakes violently, sailors and soldiers are jolted awake, thrown from their bunks onto the ground.

In one corner of the room, a semi-conscious soldier is flung from his bunk and collides with Butch, hitting his head on a nearby pole. The impact wakes him up, but he is dazed and disoriented. Meanwhile, water begins to pour into the lower deck, a result of another explosion.

Butch, a seasoned soldier, quickly assesses the situation and turns to the injured soldier. Without directly asking for his condition, he calmly asks, "You alright, mate?" Butch helps him up and together they jump into the rising water beside the bunk.

Despite his drowsiness, the soldier manages to respond, "Yeah, what's all the water?" Butch explains the situation, asking if he can walk. With Butch's assistance, the soldier nods and they make their way towards the stairs.

The scene is chaotic as soldiers scramble to make their way up the steps. But Butch stays behind with two other men to survey the damage. In the knee-deep water, Butch walks past the body of a fallen soldier, his face a mask of calmness and determination.

Suddenly, Butch notices movement in the water and quickly moves towards it. As he approaches, he sees the hand of a soldier sticking out from the water.

Without hesitation, Butch grabs the hand and flips the body over. It is Mark who has managed to survive the explosion. He is coughing and spluttering, vomiting water. Butch's face shows a mixture of surprise and relief.

"Thought I'd seen the last of you," he remarks, half-jokingly.

Mark, still coughing, responds, "Can't get rid of me that easy." Butch lifts Mark onto a top bunk bed, placing him near a large porthole.

"This must be like hell," Butch mutters to himself as he looks around. Suddenly, Butch's senses are brought back to reality as he realizes the water is rising rapidly. He quickly grabs Mark and places him on the bed, promising to come back for him. As he surveys his surroundings, he notices an injured boy-soldier slumped against a wall. Butch wades through the water to kneel beside him.

"Are you alright, son?" Butch asks, his voice filled with concern.

The boy-soldier, confused and shocked, wipes his face with a shaking hand. "What's all this blood?" he asks, his voice trembling.

Butch reassures him, "You're coming with me, champ. We're going to be alright, don't worry. I got you." With that, Butch cradles the boy-soldier and carries him through the water.

From his bunk, Mark watches as Butch climbs the stairs, carrying the boy-soldier to safety. He smiles with admiration, watching as Butch places the boy-soldier in a lifeboat that is being lowered into the water. As the boy-soldier looks back at him, Mark smiles with contentment as the young soldier is safe.

But Mark's peaceful moment is interrupted as he notices the rising water, now only inches away from his bunk. Butch's words echo in his mind.

"Told you I'd come back."

Suddenly, Butch's arm hooks over Mark and pulls him down into the water. Butch sidestrokes through the churning waves, determined to reach safety.

As they swim towards a searchlight, their only hope of rescue, Butch trudges a step below the waterline, with Mark in tow. Butch's determination and strength are clear as he struggles to keep both himself and Mark afloat.

* * *

Inside the *M24* submarine, Lieutenant Ban's hands trembled as he pulled away from the periscope, sweat dripping down his forehead. He turned to Namori, his second-in-command.

"Only wish we had more lead," Lieutenant Ban muttered, his voice filled with frustration.

"Don't worry," Namori reassured him, his tone calm and confident. "You honor the Emperor and your family would be proud."

Lieutenant Ban's face lit up, a proud smile spreading across his lips. But as he glanced down, his expression turned grave. The oxygen gauge read, "Empty."

The air was thick and suffocating inside the cramped *M24* midget submarine. The dim lighting and narrow corridors only added to the claustrophobic atmosphere. Lieutenant Ban could feel his heart racing as he thought about their current situation.

As Butch emerged from the *Kuttabul* stairs, he struggled to carry Mark's limp body. The deck of the ship was flooded with knee-deep water, making it difficult for them to move. Butch carefully made his way to the railing, his movements strained and desperate. Without hesitation, they both jumped into the murky depths of Sydney Harbour. The water was freezing, and the waves were rough, but Butch was determined to save Mark. He could hear Mark's labored breathing and the sound of the waves crashing against the ship.

"Hold on, Mark. I've got you," Butch said, his voice filled with determination. Butch's heart raced as he fought against the strong current, determined to reach safety with Mark in tow.

Butch and Mark bob in the water, their arms and legs working to keep them afloat. Above them, the bright arc lights illuminate the dark ocean, casting eerie shadows. A loud siren pierces through the air, signaling danger.

Butch glances at Mark, his concern evident. "You okay to swim?" he asks, his voice filled with worry.

Mark gives a determined nod, his eyes reflecting his determination. They kick their way away from their sinking boat, the water splashing around them. Suddenly, a small dinghy appears, its outline barely visible in the dim light. Two figures, their faces blackened, lean over the side. As the dinghy draws closer, a hand reaches out towards Butch and Mark.

Butch is pulled onto the dinghy, his muscles straining against the weight of his soaked clothes. Mark follows, his body trembling from exhaustion. As he wipes the water from his eyes, he finally sees their rescuer—Ben. A sense of relief washes over him, and a wide grin spreads across his face. He embraces his formerly timid friend in a tight hug, grateful to see him.

The ocean churns around them, its waves crashing against the sides of the dinghy. The wind howls, adding to the chaos.

Butch and Mark's hearts race as they cling to each other, grateful to have survived the deadly strike. Butch and Mark tread water as arc lights swirl atop the ocean. A warning siren blares.

Ben expertly knots the rope around the wharf, securing the dinghy in place. Butch follows suit, his strong hands effortlessly helping the two soldiers onto the solid ground. Mark, the last one to disembark, steps onto the wharf with confident stride.

The soldiers, grateful and relieved, embraced Ben in a tight hug. He stands there, grinning in surprise at their display of gratitude.

"We owe you our lives, mate," Mark says, his voice full of emotion.

Ben simply shrugs it off, "It's no big deal, really."

Butch and Mark pat Ben on the back, their admiration clear in their actions. The three of them begin to walk towards the hill, with Butch taking the lead.

As they make their way towards Garden Island, Butch turns to Mark and asks, "So, why did you tie me up and bring me onto the boat?"

Mark responds with a swift blow to Butch's head, causing him to collapse onto the ground. Ben and Mark quickly rush to his side, checking if he's okay.

"Why did you do that?" Ben asks, his tone laced with annoyance.

Mark explains, "He was asking too many questions. If he went back to the island, he would have told his mates about us, and we would be in trouble."

Together, they lift Butch and carry him up the hill towards Garden Island.

"This feels like *déjà vu*," Ben grumbles, clearly frustrated with the situation.

* * *

5.5 kms Northeast of Sydney's northern beaches

The Tasman Sea stretches out on the surface, a dark expanse that seemed to merge with the night sky. In the distance, the faint outline of land could be seen, along with the glimmer of distant lights.

Below the surface, the *M24* submarine, once a formidable vessel, now lay motionless on the ocean floor. Its exterior was riddled with giant bullet holes, evidence of a recent battle. The bow was dented, a clear sign of the damage it had endured.

Inside the *M24*, Lieutenant Ban and Namori lay face down, their bodies drenched in sweat.

In the dim light, Lieutenant Ban strained to lift his head and turned to Namori. "We should have returned to the blue swirl."

Namori gasped for breath before responding, "Maybe it was heaven?"

The two men's faces were barely visible in the low light, but their exhaustion and fear were clear. The light flickers out.

The once mighty rising sun was setting along with two brave souls.

CHAPTER 15

AFTERMATH

10 AM June 1, 1942.
Woolloomooloo Hotel

The morning sun shone brightly as Gemma, Ben, Mark, and Dot strolled along the footpath outside the pub. The Botanical Gardens were a lush green backdrop to their leisurely walk.

As they approached, Gemma spotted two young boys and called out to them, waving her hand in the air. She quickly turned to her friends and said, "I heard there's a soldier tied up in the park. Under that tree on the hill. He might need some help."

Without hesitation, the two boys looked at each other and took off in the direction of the park. Gemma led the rest of the group into the pub, passing a cleaner hosing down the footpath. The sound of a radio bulletin interrupted their conversation.

"We interrupt our regular programming for a major bulletin," announced the silver-tongued radio announcer. "Last night, the war finally hit home as twenty-one sailors and soldiers were killed on an Australian vessel in Sydney Harbour. *H.M.A.S. Kuttabul* was torpedoed by a Japanese midget submarine."

The cleaner shook his head in disbelief as he continued to hose. Gemma, Ben, and Mark's faces reflected the gravity of the terrible news, while Dot's expression showed her understanding of the situation.

"We did what we could," Gemma said, trying to comfort her friends. "At least Pop is okay."

Mark pulled Gemma aside, away from Dot and Ben. "Dot wants to come with us," he told her. "She wants to live in the future."

Gemma's grip tightened on Mark's arm. "She can't, Mark," she said firmly. "We can't guarantee her safety if she comes back. And who knows, she may not even exist in the future. That means her kids wouldn't exist either."

Mark's face fell as he realized the consequences of their actions. "And Rachel wouldn't exist," he added.

Gemma's voice softened as she looked at her friend. "She has to stay," she said, empathizing with Mark's struggle. "Think about her family, her friends, her job. They'll all wonder what happened to her. How would you feel if your daughter disappeared without a trace?"

Mark hesitated before answering, "It would haunt me for the rest of my life."

"You see?" Gemma said, placing a hand on Mark's shoulder, "We have to tell her that she can't come. It's for her own good."

Mark nodded in understanding. "I'll tell her when we get to the cove," he said, turning his head away. With heavy hearts, they continued their journey, knowing that their actions would have long-lasting consequences.

As the tram came to a halt at Watson's Bay, Gemma and Ben quickly departed, leaving Dot behind. She sat huddled by the window, dozing peacefully. Mark's expression turned grim as he approached her.

"Dot, you can't come with us," he said.

"What? Why not?" Dot asked, her eyes widening.

"You have to stay in your time," Mark replied, trying to come up with a convincing lie. "There's something important you have to do here, not in sixty years."

Dot's face fell and tears began to well up in her eyes. "But I want to see the future," she protested.

"You will, you will," Mark assured her, but the words felt hollow even to his own ears.

Frustrated and upset, Dot stormed off with Gemma chasing after her. Ben moved closer to Mark and patted him on the shoulder.

"Dude, it's for her own good," he said. "That's why all those *Star Trek* shows have rules on time travel."

Mark furrowed his brow in confusion, "What in the hell are you talking about?"

"The Temporal Time Directive," Ben explained, annoyed. "Starfleet personnel were strictly forbidden from interfering with historical events and were required to maintain the time-line and prevent any changes. It also restricted people from revealing too much about the future, to avoid causing paradoxes or altering the timeline. *Comprende?"*

Mark looked at him intensely, trying to make sense of what he was saying. "Time travel rules 101, huh? You really are a geek."

With a shake of his head, Mark turned and walked away, leaving Ben yelling after him, "You know I'm right!"

At the Harbour Beach where they journeyed to 1942, the full moon casts a soft glow over the ocean as Gemma, Ben, and Mark emerge from the darkness. They are dressed in board shorts, flippers, and goggles, ready for their underwater journey.

Ben's excitement is palpable as he proclaims, "I won't miss this old-timey place." His eyes sparkle with anticipation, and his body language radiates energy.

Gemma asks, "Why not?" Her tone suggests that she already knows the answer.

Ben's response is immediate, "The prisons, the music, those pre-historic phones." He mimics the slow movements of a circular phone dial with his hand, emphasizing his disdain for outdated technology.

Mark's guilt is evident as he admits, "I felt terrible about that. Dot was such a kind person."

Gemma's expression softens as she remembers, "But she had to go back. If she had come with us, she would never have had her daughter, who then had Rachel. They wouldn't even exist if we had changed the past."

Ben interjects, *"Temporal Time Directive,* people." He smirks, knowing he was right all along.

Mark's frustration boils over as he snaps, "Shut up!"

Gemma reaches out and gently touches Mark's arm, offering comfort and support. The three friends then place their snorkels in their mouths and dive into the water, ready to explore the underwater world beneath them.

Gemma, Mark, and Ben swam in a line, their bodies slicing through the cool water as they headed towards their destination. A mysterious, blue glow caught their attention, beckoning them closer. They exchanged nervous glances; their hands tightly intertwined as they bravely ventured towards the pulsing swirl.

As they approached, Mark's sharp eyes caught sight of something to his right. He motioned towards it, signaling to the others before they disappeared into the swirling vortex.

The trio appeared on the surface, gasping for air as they removed their gear. Weary, they scanned their surroundings, only to find themselves back in the same time period. Gemma's heart sank as she realized they had failed.

Amidst the dimly lit harbor, a ferry from the 1940s slowly emerged from behind the dark headland. A few passengers waited onboard; their voices drowned out by the muted bell signaling the ferry's departure.

Gemma's frustration boiled over as she exclaimed, "Oh no, we're back at the same time!"

Mark, still catching his breath, added, "I saw something near the tide marker before we swam into the swirl."

"What was it?" Ben asked, his curiosity piqued.

"It looked like an old, mechanical box with dials and gadgets," Mark replied.

Without hesitation, Gemma pointed downwards and declared, "Let's go check it out. Maybe it's the key to getting us back home!"

The trio quickly donned their gear and dove back into the water, determined to unravel the mystery of the time-traveling device.

Mark dives confidently towards the device, his companions Ben and Gemma following closely behind. As they approach, they can see the device wedged in a rock next to the tide marker pole. Their eyes widen in awe as they take in the mysterious contraption. Without hesitation, Mark reaches out and changes the dial, a date now appearing on its surface: "4, OCTOBER 2007." As his fingers make contact, the device begins to pulse and the glow emitting from it transforms into a deep, mesmerizing blue.

Gemma gives a thumbs up, her excitement clear in her wide grin, and points towards the source of the blue light. Without hesitation, she dives towards it, beckoning for her friends to follow. With determination in their eyes, Mark and Ben grab onto Gemma's hand and join her in the water, disappearing into the pulsating unknown.

The sound of a motor grew louder and louder, its muffled growl filling the air. Gemma, Mark, and Ben appeared from the depths of the water in perfect synchrony, gasping for air.

As they tried to catch their breath, their eyes widened in fear as they spotted a jet ski speeding towards them. The pilot, a young man in his twenties, and his passenger frantically tried to avoid a collision.

"Fuu—" Mark's voice was drowned out by the roar of the engine. The trio quickly dove back under the water just as the jet ski zipped over them, causing a loud thud as it hit something.

The passenger cursed as they realized they had hit something. "Shit! We hit 'em, go back!" The jet ski turned around and slowed down, the pilot and passenger scrambling around the boat in a panic.

After a few moments, Gemma, Mark, and Ben resurfaced, gasping for air. The pilot let out a sigh of relief.

"Ohhh! We thought we hit you." His voice was filled with genuine concern.

"You did," Ben replied, holding up his shredded backpack, "My backpack saved us! Hey dude, what's the date today?"

The pilot checked his watch and replied, "Man, it's October fourth or fifth."

"2007, right?" Ben asked, his eyes lighting up with excitement.

"Of course, dude. Yeah, 2007." The pilot seemed taken aback by the question.

Ben pumped his fist in the air, a wide smile spreading across his face as Mark and Gemma beamed. The passenger, however, looked less than pleased.

"They're pretty happy, considering we nearly killed 'em," she pointed out.

"We should get to Pop's place," Gemma suggested.

"Man, they're never gonna believe us."

"I don't believe it—and I was there!" Mark chimed in with a smile.

This was a moment they would never forget, a moment of pure adrenaline and fear that would become a story to tell for years to come. The sun was shining, the water was crystal clear, and they were all safe and sound.

CHAPTER 16

RECALL

Morning sunlight filtered through the trees, casting dappled shadows on the quiet street. Mark's Mazda Hatchback rolled to a stop in front of the Bondi California bungalow. With a sense of urgency, Mark, Gemma, and Ben leapt out of the car and charged towards the house. Mark quickly opened the door and the trio burst into the hallway.

"Hey, Pop—Gran? Are you there?" Mark called out, his voice echoing through the empty space.

They hurried down the hallway, their footsteps echoing against the hardwood floors. The lounge and kitchen were still ahead, but there was no sign of their grandparents.

Gemma, Mark, and Ben raced into the backyard, their hearts pounding with worry.

"Pop, Gran? Where are you!" Gemma's voice trembled with concern.

"They have to be here. Pop was okay when we left him," Mark's words trailed off as they searched the yard, their eyes scanning every inch for a sign of their missing grandparents.

"I hate to say it, but we never saw him after we went to the pub. He was still tied up!" Ben's voice was filled with regret.

Gemma's mind raced as she tried to figure out where their grandparents could be.

"I sent those kids to find him," she muttered, her voice barely above a whisper.

The trio exchanged worried glances before marching back into the house. With each step, the sense of foreboding grew stronger. What had happened to their beloved grandparents? The once familiar house now felt cold and empty, adding to their anxiety. But they had to stay strong and keep searching, hoping to find their grandparents safe and sound.

Mark rushes down the hallway and bursts into his grandparents' bedroom. Gemma and Ben follow, walking towards the front door. Gemma's eyes catch a glimpse of a shadow through the glass. Suddenly, the door swings open and she is faced with her startled grandfather, Kevin, who was once known as "Butch." Without hesitation, Gemma throws herself into her grandfather's arms, overcome with relief. She sobs uncontrollably, clinging to him as if he had just been saved from the electric chair. Kevin gently pats her head and wraps his aging arms around her. Mark joins in, hugging and kissing his Pop on the head. Kevin is taken aback by Mark's display of affection and a tear escapes his eye. Ben stands behind Mark, grinning from ear to ear.

Gemma's sobs continue as she explains to her grandfather, "We came in, and you weren't here. We thought you were dead."

Kevin wipes away his own tears, confused by her reaction. "Dead? I was at Eric's place next door, testing his home brew! Why did you think I was dead?"

Mark and Ben jump up and down excitedly, clapping and pumping their fists in the air.

Gemma stays calm, but her eyes dart nervously between Mark and Ben. "Pop," she begins, her voice trembling. "What I am about to tell you may sound unbelievable, but you have to believe me. You know I never lie to you."

Kevin takes hold of her arms, concern etched on his face, "Gemma, what's wrong?" he asks, his voice filled with worry.

"Pop. Do you remember being kidnapped by three young people on the night you were supposed to board the *Kuttabul* in 1942?" Gemma's words hang in the air, the tension is palpable.

"No, Gem, you know what happened. I was mugged," Kevin responds, his confusion growing. "What are you saying, Gemma?"

"Pop. We time traveled," Gemma reveals, her voice barely above a whisper. "We went to your house, to a party, on the night you were supposed to board the *Kuttabul* and we kidnapped you."

"It's true, Pop," Mark chimes in, eager to support Gemma's story.

Kevin releases Gemma, disappointment clear on his face. "Oh Gem, I never thought you would take drugs," he says, shaking his head.

"She doesn't take drugs, Pop," Mark interjects. "You know she's a control freak."

"You haven't been on that hashishi hydrochloric acid, have you?" Kevin asks, his voice laced with concern.

"We stopped you from boarding the *Kuttabul*. The Japs torpedoed it," Mark declares, his eyes wide with excitement.

"No!" Kevin exclaims, his face turning red with anger. "I'm betting it's the hashishi. Stick to liquor, I reckon."

"Yeah, it only stuffs your liver," Mark retorts. "Look, we went back through a time portal. We visited 1942!"

"Only Dr. Spark and Captain Curtain can time travel," Kevin argues.

"It's Mr. Spock and Captain Kirk," Gemma corrects him, with a resigned sigh.

"Pop, can you promise not to mention this Kuttabul incident to Grandma?" Gemma asks, a pleading look in her eyes. "I want to talk to her, just the two of us. A girl-to-girl chat always gets results."

Kevin agrees but reminds Gemma to be careful with her words. He knows how much his wife cares for their grandchildren. Gemma looks at Mark and Ben, who are disappointed that they won't be a part of the upcoming conversation.

Gemma hesitantly approaches Nell in the kitchen of Bentley House. She takes a deep breath and reaches for Nell's hand, her palms sweating with nerves. Nell looks at her curiously, waiting for Gemma to speak.

"Gran, I need to ask you something," Gemma says, her voice trembling.

Nell's eyebrows rise in surprise, but she stays silent, waiting for Gemma to continue.

"Do you remember the night the *Kuttabul* was torpedoed?" Gemma asks, struggling to find the right words. "At Pop's party, there were three strangers there, around my age. Do you remember meeting them?"

Nell pauses, her mind traveling back in time. She settles back in her chair, her eyes distant.

"Honey, that was over sixty years ago," she says, her voice soft. "My memory is still sharp, but that's a lifetime ago."

Gemma looks down, disappointment clear in her expression. She had hoped Nell would remember the three strangers, but it seemed like a lost cause.

"Take your time," Gemma says, trying to hide her disappointment.

Nell tilts her head back and takes a deep breath, lost in thought. After a moment, she shakes her head. "I can't recall any young strangers at the party," she says, her voice apologetic.

Gemma's heart sinks, but she doesn't give up. She knows she needs to tell Nell the truth, even if it hurts. She looks at Nell with tenderness and stands up, wrapping her arms around her in a hug. "Gran, there's something I need to tell you," she says, her voice filled with emotion.

Nell looks at her with concern, waiting for Gemma to speak. But at that moment, Gemma decides to spare Nell the pain and keep her secret for now.

"It can wait for another time," she says, squeezing Nell's hand. "I love you, Gran. I love you so much."

Nell's eyes soften, and she smiles at Gemma. She then asks for Mark to come in, wanting to talk to him. Gemma nods, understanding her grandmother's need for support. She leaves the kitchen, leaving Nell alone with her thoughts.

Mark enters the room and takes a seat next to Nell. He greets her with a casual, "What's up, Gran?"

Nell's face at once turns serious, her expression revealing the weight of her words.

"I know you blame your Pop for the car crash that took your parents' lives," Nell says, her tone somber. Mark's eyes widen in surprise, but he stays silent, waiting for her to continue. "Do you know what caused the argument that day?" Nell asks, her eyes searching Mark's face. He shakes his head, clueless.

Nell takes a deep breath before revealing the truth.

"Your Grandfather gently mentioned to your Dad that we wanted to take care of you both, to give your parents a break," she says, her voice tinged with sadness.

Mark leans forward in his chair, intrigued by this new information.

"But your Dad became angry, and your Pop tried to drop the subject," Nell continues. "That's when the accident happened."

Mark's mind races, trying to process what he's hearing. He feels a wave of guilt wash over him, realizing how wrong he had been about his Pop all these years.

"Gran, I'm sorry," Mark says, his voice filled with remorse. "I now know that Pop is and always has been a caring person."

Nell nods, her eyes softening at Mark's apology.

Mark leans back in his chair, the weight of his longheld resentment lifting from his shoulders. He grins at his grandmother, grateful for her honesty and the new perspective it has given him.

Morning sunlight streamed through the trees, casting a warm glow on the front yard of Bentley House. Mark stepped out of the door and made his way to the lawn where Ben and Gemma were already waiting.

"What did Gran want?" Gemma asked.

Mark hesitated before answering, "She spoke to me about the accident."

Gemma nodded, understanding the weight of the conversation.

"And you're cool with Pop?" she asked, wanting to make sure Mark was okay.

"Yeah," Mark replied, "I've been a bit hard on the old bastard."

Gemma nodded again, knowing how Mark had been struggling with his relationship with their grandfather.

"What about your talk?" Mark asked, concerned, "Did she remember us being there?"

Gemma's face fell, "No, it's too long ago."

Mark couldn't believe it. "We just can't let it go like that. It happened, Gemma. I can't believe we went through all of that for nothing!" He started to pace, frustration and anger building inside of him.

"I know, Mark," Gemma said, placing a comforting hand on his arm. "But people forget after six decades. And it wasn't for nothing. We've changed, Mark. It changed everything."

Mark stopped pacing and looked at Gemma. "What do you mean?"

She squeezed his hand. "You stood up for me in the pub. You saved me from those sailor perverts, and you saved Pop from drowning. And he saved you."

Mark nodded, acknowledging her observation.

"And you cared about Dot," Gemma continued. "You put her before your own selfish needs for the first time. I'm so proud of you. You've changed, Mr. Bentley."

Mark's demeanor softened. "Maybe, in some ways."

Gemma turned to Ben. "And you, Ben. You helped those soldiers. Before, you would never have gotten into a fight. But that's exactly what you did. You showed guts, courage."

Mark playfully ruffled Ben's hair, causing him to blush with embarrassment.

"That's Purple Haze stuff, Ben!" Gemma exclaimed.

"Purple Heart, Gem," Ben corrected, "And that's an American medal. It's the Victoria Cross in Australia."

Gemma brushed it off. "Whatever. Ben, that's one of the bravest things I've ever seen. You were amazing."

Mark chimed in, "Dude, you are a dead-set legend."

"And not only have you changed," Mark added, "You've turned into a kick-ass Vin Diesel kind of guy." Mark and Gemma playfully bowed at Ben's feet before patting him on the back.

"You know somethin'?" Ben said, "The oldies are the key to who we are."

"That's pretty deep, dude," Mark said, "You know what I realized?"

Gemma and Ben looked at him expectantly.

"How much I missed dacking Ben!" Mark exclaimed, diving at his mate and playfully trying to pull his pants down.

"What are you, like a five-year-old? Stop!! Stop!!" Ben yelled, trying to push Mark off. Gemma joined in on the fun, diving on top of the boys as they continued to frolic in the front yard.

* * *

One week had passed since Mark's encounter with the strange girl at the beach. As he stepped out of a Campbell Parade surf shop, he turned to say goodbye to Karl, the shop owner standing by the door. Mark promised to return the next day to pick up his wetsuit for surfing.

As he made his way down Campbell Parade, Mark was suddenly interrupted by a bump from behind. Turning around, he saw a man wearing board shorts, a t-shirt, and thongs. It was Professor John Bentley, who sported a wry grin. Attached to his back was a see-through backpack, containing all sorts of beach gear along with a top-hat.

Mark was perplexed by the man's top hat, but before he could question further, the Professor had already moved on. Mark continued walking, taking in the sights and sounds of the bustling street. Suddenly, he spotted Rachel, the jogger he had met the other day at the beach. She was walking with her head down, fixated on her phone.

"Rachel!" Mark exclaimed, surprised to see her again. "Do you remember me?"

Rachel turned and smiled widely at the sight of Mark. "Of course, I do," she replied. "You put on quite a show for us in the water that day."

Mark felt embarrassed, but Rachel's compliment made him feel a little better. "Well, I wasn't exactly a willing participant," he admitted.

Rachel chuckled. "It was a nice distraction, though," she said.

Mark's curiosity was piqued. "Listen, did you have a relative who lived in Woolloomooloo about sixty years ago?"

"Oh, my grandma, Dot," Rachel replied. "Why, did you bump into her?"

Mark paused, collecting his thoughts. Rachel raised her eyebrows, waiting for his response.

"I was looking through some old photos the other day, and I saw a girl who looked just like you," Mark explained. "My grandparents said her name was Dot and she lived in 'The Loo' The suburb, not the toilet."

Rachel laughed. "I knew what you meant," she said. "That's crazy, I'll have to tell her."

Mark was flabbergasted. "She's still alive?"

"Yep, eighty-two and going strong," Rachel replied. "What were your grandparents' names?"

"Kevin and Nell Bentley," Mark answered.

"Well, my grandma was Nell Brand back then." Rachel grinned. "Would you like to go out for a drink sometime?"

Mark's heart skipped a beat. "Cool, yeah, I'd love to," he replied.

"Great, how about eight tomorrow night at my place?" Rachel suggested, pulling out a pen and paper from her bag. She scribbled down her address and handed it to Mark.

Mark couldn't contain his excitement. "Tomorrow, your place," he repeated.

"Yep, and you can meet my grandma when you visit. She lives with us," Rachel said with a smile.

Mark couldn't believe it. "Great, Dot's still alive," he muttered in disbelief. As he turned to walk away, he looked back at Rachel, who waved at him with a smile. Mark couldn't wait for their date tomorrow, and to meet the woman who looked so much like her. He couldn't believe how much his life had changed in just one week.

* * *

The sun was beginning to set as Nell entered her bedroom. She walked slowly towards her cupboard; her eyes fixed on the old wooden box sitting on top. With a gentle hand, she lifted the box and placed it delicately on the bed. Her gaze lingered on the box for a moment before she sat down, her movements filled with a sense of reverence.

Carefully, Nell opened the box, revealing its contents.

Inside were memories from the war: faded photos from WWII, Butch's medals and insignias. Her fingers trembled as she picked up two photos of Butch. In the first one, he was surrounded by his army mates, their arms wrapped around each other in a display of camaraderie. They were dressed casually in military shorts and singlets, a stark contrast to the second photo where Butch stood tall and proud in his dress uniform and slouch hat. Nell smiled at the picture, her love for Butch evident in her eyes.

Gently placing the photos back in the box, Nell let out a sigh, her emotions overwhelming her. As she reached the bottom of the box, her hand brushed against something familiar and out of place. It was Mark's old mobile phone, its antique condition a reminder of the sixty-five years that had passed.

Just then, Kevin appeared at the door. Nell looked up at him, her eyes filled with a mix of sadness and longing. Without a word, Kevin knew what she was thinking.

"Are you going to tell them?" Nell asked, her voice barely above a whisper.

Kevin hesitated, then nodded in agreement.

It was time.

CHAPTER 17

WIZARDS

Rachel's house was nestled in a quiet neighborhood, the moon casting shadows on the neat lawns and white picket fences. Mark's car, a sleek Mazda 3, pulled up to the curb and he stepped out confidently. He strode up to the door and knocked, but there was no answer. Frowning, he knocked again, this time with more urgency. The door creaked open slowly to reveal a frail, eighty-two-year-old woman. Mark's heart skipped a beat.

"Dot—is that you?" Mark asked, his voice full of surprise and disbelief.

"Yes, it is. Who are you?" Dot replied, her voice laced with curiosity.

Mark stumbled over his words, "Oh, uh, I'm sorry. My name is Mark. I'm here to take Rachel out."

Dot's eyes widened in recognition. "Oh yes, dear. She told me about you. Come in." She stepped aside to let Mark in, her gaze lingering on him a little too keenly.

Mark followed Dot into the living room, taking in the cozy furniture and family photos on the walls. Dot gestured for him to sit on the couch, while she settled into a single seat across from him.

"Dot, do you recognize me?" Mark asked, his voice trembling with nerves.

"Should I?" Dot replied, her expression sceptical.

Mark took a deep breath, "Here goes. This might sound strange, but it was sixty-five years ago at Butch's party, in Woolloomooloo. Do you remember me from that party?"

Dot furrowed her brow, clearly doubtful.

"I was there with my sister, Gemma, and my mate, Ben. We all ended up sleeping overnight in the Botanical Gardens—Butch included. It was right after we kidnapped him. Remember?" Mark continued, hoping to jog her memory.

But Dot's expression remained sceptical, and at that moment, Rachel burst through the door, apologizing for being late.

"Hi Mark, I'm sorry. You've met Grandma, obviously," Rachel said, gesturing towards Dot. "I'm going to quickly change, and then we can head out. You two can chat about your grandparents while I get ready."

As Rachel disappeared down the hallway, Mark took a seat again, feeling a sense of discomfort in the air.

Dot decided to make small talk and asked, "Who are your grandparents?"

"They're Kevin and Nell Bentley. Do you know them?" Mark asked, hoping for some kind of connection.

Dot hesitated; her expression pensive. "No, I can't say that I do."

Mark's heart sank, and he realized that Dot didn't remember anything from that party all those years ago. He stood up, feeling disappointed and unsure.

"Well, no worries. I'll just wait outside in the car for Rachel," he said, making his way to the door. He paused, as if wanting to say something, but ultimately decided against it and opened the door to leave.

Mark strolls down the driveway, his brow furrowed in confusion. As he approaches the car, a familiar voice drifts towards him.

"Did you ever finish that tale about hobbits and wizards in Middle Earth?" Dot's voice rings out. "I always believed in you."

A broad grin spreads across Mark's face as he turns to face Dot. Their shared secret passes between them, unspoken.

Soon, Rachel joins them, sliding up to Dot and placing a gentle kiss on her grandmother's cheek. She then turns to Mark, "Did she reminisce about old times?" Rachel asks.

Mark's grin widens. "I did most of the reminiscing," he replies. "We've got loads to catch up on."

Rachel's anticipation is palpable. "Oh? I've been looking forward to this," she says eagerly. "So where are we going?"

With Rachel's arm linked through his, Mark leads the way towards his car. They both seem completely at ease, a sense of contentment radiating from them. Mark can't help but flash a cheeky grin at Rachel.

"We'll go for a drink at the Bondi," he says, pausing for emphasis. "And by the way, do you like snorkeling?"

Rachel's eyes light up with excitement. "Yeah, I do," she replies. "It feels like time stands still while I'm down there."

Mark's grin grows even wider. "That's not even the half of it," he says, his voice full of anticipation.

Hand in hand, they continue towards the car, each step bringing them closer to their upcoming adventure together.

THE END

Author's Notes

This story is fictional, but it is based on factual events.

On May 30, 1942 at twilight, a toy-like plane was launched from the deck of a large Japanese submarine, twelve kilometers from Sydney's northern beaches. The plane's pilot diagrammed the position of allied ships in the Harbour. He then crash-landed near the large Japanese submarine off Manly and relayed his findings to his Captain. The next evening three midget submarines launched the only successful World War Two raid on Sydney.

Twenty-one brave men aboard *H.M.A.S. Kuttabul* and six fearless Japanese submariners paid the ultimate sacrifice on that fateful night. This novel is dedicated to their bravery.

About the Author

Australian author Graham Bottomley crafts stories of love, sci-fi, adventure, and history, inspired by his Sydney upbringing and his adoptive parents' legacy. His debut novel, *Time on the Harbour*, honors his father's WWII experiences. Now based on the Gold Coast, Graham continues to create captivating tales across genres and eras.

EXPLORE NEW HORIZONS WITH US AS
WE SAIL ONTO SHORES OF LATEST PROD-
UCTS, EVENTS, GREAT TITLES, AND BE-
YOND.

VISIT US:
WWW.OCEANIACOM.COM

OCEANIACOM PRESS